T0169433

Caress of Darkness

A Dark Pleasures Novella

By Julie Kenner

1001 Dark Nights

EVIL EYE
CONCEPTS

Caress of Darkness
A Dark Pleasures Novella
By Julie Kenner

Copyright 2014 Julie Kenner
ISBN: 978-1-682305775

Foreword: Copyright 2014 M. J. Rose

Published by Evil Eye Concepts, Incorporated

All rights reserved. No part of this book may be reproduced, scanned, or distributed in any printed or electronic form without permission. Please do not participate in or encourage piracy of copyrighted materials in violation of the author's rights.

This is a work of fiction. Names, places, characters and incidents are the product of the author's imagination and are fictitious. Any resemblance to actual persons, living or dead, events or establishments is solely coincidental.

Sign up for the 1001 Dark Nights Newsletter
and be entered to win a Tiffany Key necklace.

There's a contest every month!

Go to www.1001DarkNights.com to subscribe.

As a bonus, all subscribers will receive a free
1001 Dark Nights story
The First Night
by Lexi Blake & M.J. Rose

One Thousand and One Dark Nights

Once upon a time, in the future…

*I was a student fascinated with stories and learning.
I studied philosophy, poetry, history, the occult, and
the art and science of love and magic. I had a vast
library at my father's home and collected thousands
of volumes of fantastic tales.*

*I learned all about ancient races and bygone
times. About myths and legends and dreams of all
people through the millennium. And the more I read
the stronger my imagination grew until I discovered
that I was able to travel into the stories… to actually
become part of them.*

*I wish I could say that I listened to my teacher
and respected my gift, as I ought to have. If I had, I
would not be telling you this tale now.
But I was foolhardy and confused, showing off
with bravery.*

*One afternoon, curious about the myth of the
Arabian Nights, I traveled back to ancient Persia to
see for myself if it was true that every day Shahryar
(Persian: راىردش, "king") married a new virgin, and then
sent yesterday's wife to be beheaded. It was written
and I had read, that by the time he met Scheherazade,
the vizier's daughter, he'd killed one thousand
women.*

Something went wrong with my efforts. I arrived in the midst of the story and somehow exchanged places with Scheherazade — a phenomena that had never occurred before and that still to this day, I cannot explain.

Now I am trapped in that ancient past. I have taken on Scheherazade's life and the only way I can protect myself and stay alive is to do what she did to protect herself and stay alive.

Every night the King calls for me and listens as I spin tales. And when the evening ends and dawn breaks, I stop at a point that leaves him breathless and yearning for more. And so the King spares my life for one more day, so that he might hear the rest of my dark tale.

As soon as I finish a story... I begin a new one... like the one that you, dear reader, have before you now.

Chapter 1

"Who the fuck are you?"

I jump, startled by the voice—deep and male and undeniably irritated—that echoes across the forest of boxes scattered throughout my father's Upper East Side antique store.

"Who am I?" I repeat as I stand and search the shadows for the intruder. "Who the hell are you?"

There is more bravado in my voice than I feel, especially when I finally see the man who has spoken. He is standing in the shadows near the front door—a door that I am damn sure I locked after putting the *Closed* sign in the window and settling in for a long night of inventory and packing.

He is tall, well over six feet, with a lean, muscular build that is accentuated by the faded jeans that hug his thighs and the simple white T-shirt that reveals muscled arms sleeved with tattoos.

His casual clothes, inked skin, and close-shaved head hint at danger and rebellion, but those traits are contrasted by a commanding, almost elegant, presence that seems to both fill the room and take charge of it. This is a man who would be equally at ease in a tux as a T-shirt. A man who expects the world to bend to his will, and if it doesn't comply, he will go out and bend it himself.

I see that confidence most potently in his face, all sharp lines and angles that blend together into a masterpiece now dusted with the shadow of a late afternoon beard. He has the kind of eyes that miss nothing, and right now they are hard and assessing. They are softened, however, by long, dark lashes that most women would kill for.

His mouth is little more than a hard slash across his features, but I see a hint of softness, and when I find myself wondering how those lips would feel against my skin, I realize that I have been staring and yank myself firmly from my reverie.

"I asked you a question," I snap, more harshly than I intended. "Who are you, and how did you get in here?"

"Raine," he says, striding toward me. "Rainer Engel. And I walked in through the front door."

"I locked it." I wipe my now-sweaty hands on my dusty yoga pants.

"The fact that I'm inside suggests otherwise."

He has crossed the store in long, efficient strides, and now stands in front of me. I catch his scent, all musk and male, sin and sensuality, and feel an unwelcome ache between my thighs.

Not unwelcome because I don't like sex. On the contrary, I'd have to label myself a fan, and an overenthusiastic one at that. Because the truth is that I've spent too many nights in the arms of too many strangers trying to fill some void in myself.

I say "some void" because I don't really know what I'm searching for. A connection, I guess, but at the same time I'm scared of finding one and ending up hurt, which is why I shy from traditional "my friend has a friend" kind of dating, and spend more time than I should in bars and clubs. And that means that while I might be enjoying a series of really good lays, I'm not doing anything more than using sex as a Band-Aid.

At least, that is what my therapist, Kelly, back home in Austin says. And since I'm a lawyer and not a shrink, I'm going to have to take her word on that.

"We're closed," I say firmly. Or, rather, I intend to say firmly.

In fact, my voice comes out thin, suggesting a question rather than a command.

Not that my tone matters. The man—*Raine*—seems entirely uninterested in what I have to say.

He cocks his head slightly to one side, as if taking my measure, and if the small curve of that sensual mouth is any indication, he likes what he sees. I prop a hand on my hip and stare back defiantly. I know what I look like—and I know that with a few exceptions, men tend to go stupid when I dial it up.

The ratty law school T-shirt I'm wearing is tight, accenting breasts that I'd cursed in high school, but that had become a boon once I started college and realized that my ample tits, slender waist, and long legs added up to a combination that made guys drool. Add in wavy blonde hair and green eyes and I've got the kind of cheerleader-esque good looks that make so many of the good old boy lawyers in Texas think that I've got cotton candy for brains.

And believe me when I say that I'm not shy about turning their misogynistic stereotype to my advantage, both in the courtroom and out of it.

"You're Callie." His voice conveys absolute certainty, as if his inspection confirmed one of the basic facts of the universe. Which, since I *am* Callie, I guess it did. But how the hell he knows who I am is beyond me.

"Your father talks about you a lot," Raine says, apparently picking up on my confusion. His eyes rake over me as he speaks, and my skin prickles with awareness, as potent as if his fingertip had stroked me. "A lawyer who lives in Texas with the kind of looks that make a father nervous, balanced by sharp, intelligent eyes that reassure him that she's not going to do anything stupid."

"You know my father."

"I know your father," he confirms.

"And he told you that about me?"

"The lawyer part. The rest I figured out all on my own." One corner of his mouth curves up. "I have eyes, after all." Those eyes are currently aimed at my chest, and I say a silent thank you to whoever decided that padded bras were a good thing because otherwise he would certainly see how hard and tight my nipples have become.

"University of Texas School of Law. Good school." He lifts his gaze from my chest to my face, and the heat I see in those ice-blue eyes seems to seep under my skin, melting me a bit from the inside out. "Very good."

I lick my lips, realizing that my mouth has gone uncomfortably dry. I've been working as an assistant district attorney for the last two years. I've gotten used to being the one in charge of a room. And right now, I'm feeling decidedly off-kilter, part of me wanting to pull him close, and the other wanting to run as far and as fast from him as I can.

Since neither option is reasonable at the moment, I simply take a step back, then find myself trapped by the glass jewelry case, now pressing against my ass.

I clear my throat. "Listen, Mr. Engel, if you're looking for my father—"

"I am, and I apologize for snapping at you when I came in, but I was surprised to see that the shop was closed, and when I saw someone other than Oliver moving inside, I got worried."

"I closed early so that I could work without being interrupted."

A hint of a smile plays at his mouth. "In that case, I'll also apologize for interrupting. But Oliver asked me to come by when I got back in town. I'm anxious to discuss the amulet that he's located."

"Oh." I don't know why I'm surprised. He obviously hadn't come into the store looking for me. And yet for some reason the fact that I've suddenly become irrelevant rubs me the wrong way.

Clearly, I need to get a grip, and I paste on my best customer service smile. "I'm really sorry, but my dad's not here."

"No? I told him I'd come straight over." I can hear the irritation in his voice. "He knows how much I want this piece—how much I'm willing to pay. If he's made arrangements to sell it to another—"

"No." The word is fast and firm and entirely unexpected. "It's not like that. My dad doesn't play games with clients."

"That's true. He doesn't." His brow creases as he looks around the shop, taking in the open boxes, half filled with inventory, the colored sticky notes I've been using to informally assign items to numbered boxes, and the general disarray of the space. "Callie, what's happened to your father?"

It is the way he says my name that loosens my tongue. Had he simply asked the question, I probably would have told him that he could come back in the morning and we'd search the computerized inventory for the piece he's looking for. But there is something so intimate about my name on his lips that I can't help but answer honestly.

"My dad had a stroke last week." My voice hitches as I speak, and I look off toward the side of the store, too wrecked to meet his eyes directly.

"Oh, Callie." He steps closer and takes my hand, and I'm surprised to find that I not only don't pull away, but that I actually have to fight the urge to pull our joint hands close to my heart.

"I didn't know," he says. "I'm so sorry. How is he doing?"

"N-not very well." I suck in a breath and try to gather myself, but it's just so damn hard. My mom walked out when I was four, saying that being a mother was too much responsibility, and ever since I've been my dad's entire world. It's always amazed me that he didn't despise me. But he really doesn't. He says that I was a gift, and I know it's true because I have seen and felt it every day of my life.

Whatever the cause of my disconnect with men, it doesn't harken back to my dad, a little fact that I know fascinates my shrink, though she's too much the professional to flat out tell me as much.

"Does he have decent care? Do you need any referrals? Any help financially?" Raine is crouching in front of me, and I realize that I have sunk down, so that my butt is on the cold tile floor and I am hugging my knees.

I shake my head, too dazed to realize this stranger is apparently offering to help pay my dad's medical bills. "We're fine. He's got great care and great insurance. He's just—" I break off as my voice cracks. *"Shit."*

"Hey, it's okay. Breathe now. That's it, just breathe." He presses his hands to my shoulders, and his face is just inches away. His eyes are wide and safe and warm, and I want to slide into them. To just disappear into a place where there are neither worries nor responsibilities. Where someone strong will hold me and take care of me and make everything bad disappear.

But that's impossible, and so I draw another breath in time with his words and try once again to formulate a coherent thought. "He's—he's got good doctors, really. But he's not lucid. And this is my dad. I mean, Oliver Sinclair hasn't gone a day in his life without an opinion or a witticism."

I feel the tears well in my eyes and I swipe them away with a brusque brush of my thumb. "And it kills me because I can look at him and it breaks my heart to know that he must have all this stuff going on inside his head that he just can't say, and— and—"

But I can't get the words out, and I feel the tears snaking down my cheeks, and dammit, dammit, *dammit*, I do not want to lose it in front of this man—this stranger who doesn't feel like a stranger.

His grip on my shoulders tightens and he leans toward me.

And then—oh, dear god—his lips are on mine and they are as warm and soft as I'd imagined and he's kissing me so gently and so sweetly that all my worries are just melting away and I'm limp in his arms.

"Shhh. It's okay." His voice washes over me, as gentle and calming as a summer rain. "Everything's going to be okay."

I breathe deep, soothed by the warm sensuality of this stranger's golden voice. Except he isn't a stranger. I may not have met him before today, but somehow, here in his arms, I *know* him.

And that, more than anything, comforts me.

Calmer, I tilt my head back and meet his eyes. It is a soft moment and a little sweet—but it doesn't stay that way. It changes in the space of a glance. In the instant of a heartbeat. And what started out as gentle comfort transforms into fiery heat.

I don't know which of us moves first. All I know is that I have to claim him and be claimed by him. That I have to taste him—consume him. Because in some essential way that I don't fully understand, I know that only this man can quell the need burning inside me, and I lose myself in the hot intensity of his mouth upon mine. Of his tongue demanding entrance, and his lips, hard and demanding, forcing me to give everything he wants to take.

I am limp against him, felled by the onslaught of erotic sparks that his kisses have scattered through me. I am lost in the sensation of his hands stroking my back. Of his chest pressed against my breasts.

But it isn't until I realize that he has pulled me into his lap and that I can feel the hard demand of his erection against my rear that I force myself to escape this sensual reality and scramble backward out of his embrace.

"I'm sorry," I say, my breath coming too hard.

"Callie—" The need I hear in his voice reflects my own, and I clench my hands into fists as I fight against the instinct to move back into his arms.

"No." I don't understand what's happening—this instant heat, like a match striking gasoline. I've never reacted to a man this way before. My skin feels prickly, as if I've been caught in a lightning storm. His scent is all over me. And the taste of him lingers on my mouth.

And oh, dear god, I'm wet, my body literally aching with need, with a primal desire for him to just rip my clothes off and take me right there on the hard, dusty floor.

He's triggered a wildness in me that I don't understand—and my reaction scares the hell out of me.

"You need to go," I say, and I am astonished that my words are both measured and articulate, as if I'm simply announcing that it is closing time to a customer.

He stays silent, but I shake my head anyway, and hold up a

finger as if in emphasis.

"No," I say, in response to nothing. "I don't know anything about this amulet. And now you really need to leave. Please," I add. "Please, Raine. I need you to go."

For a moment he only looks at me. Then he nods, a single tilt of his head in acknowledgment. "All right," he says very softly. "I'll go. But I'm not ever leaving you again."

I stand frozen, as if his inexplicable words have locked me in place. He turns slowly and strides out of the shop without looking back. And when the door clicks into place behind him and I am once more alone, I gulp in air as tears well in my eyes again.

I rub my hands over my face, forgiving myself for this emotional miasma because of all the shit that's happened with my dad. Of course I'm a wreck; what daughter wouldn't be?

Determined to get a grip, I follow his path to the door, then hold onto the knob. I'd come over intending to lock it. But now I want to yank it open and beg him to return.

It's an urge I fight. It's just my grief talking. My fear that I'm about to lose my father, the one person in all the world who is close to me, and so I have clung to a stranger in a desperate effort to hold fast to something.

That, at least, is what my shrink would say. *You're fabricating a connection in order to fill a void. It's what you do, Callie. It's what you've always done when lonely and afraid.*

I nod, telling myself I agree with Kelly's voice in my head.

And I do.

Because I am lonely.

And I am afraid of losing my dad.

But that's not the whole of it. Because there's something else that I'm afraid of, too, though I cannot put my finger on it. A strange sense of something coming. Something dark. Something bad.

And what scares me most is the ridiculous, unreasonable fear that I have just pushed away the one person I need to survive whatever is waiting for me out there in the dark.

Chapter 2

He could still taste the sweetness of her lips, and dear god, he wanted more.

Wanted everything. *Wanted her.*

The irony, of course, was that he hadn't intended to kiss her in the first place, even though from the moment she'd looked at him with those sparkling green eyes it had seemed as if he'd known her forever. But when the tears had welled in her eyes, he knew that he would have done anything to ease her grief.

The kiss had been tender. Almost sweet. But there was nothing sweet about the way he was feeling now. Bottom line?

Raine wanted Callie Sinclair. Craved her. Hungered for her.

Hell, he fucking yearned for her, and that was simply not a feeling he was used to having. Hadn't been for a very, very long time.

Oh, sure, he'd gotten off often enough. Lost himself in a woman. In the feel of her body against his. There was power in the claiming of a willing female, in that hard, rough ride that erased the world, at least for those few singular moments as the sensation built and climax approached.

And when the inevitable explosion came, he'd lose himself in the sharp oblivion that mimicked the death he sought again and again, and yet this death was forged in pleasure and not pain.

But that was all he wanted or needed—just that physical connection to remind him that no matter how dead he might feel on the inside—no matter how hard he chased that escape and no matter how many times he burned—this body still functioned and he still had a job to do.

Because if he could fuck, then he could fucking well survive another day, another year, another century.

Shit.

He ran his fingers over his close-cropped hair and told himself to get a grip. An ironic lecture since he stood like a criminal in the shadows across the street from Sinclair's Antiques, his eyes trained on the now-locked door.

Thank goodness he'd dismissed Dennis, Phoenix Security's driver, telling him to go ahead and simply be on call in case Raine needed him later. He hardly wanted to explain to the eager twenty-three-year-old why the hell he was standing like an idiot, waiting for just another glimpse of this woman who'd gotten so deep under his skin.

Christ, he was pathetic. For millennia he'd not been distracted by a woman. Not since he'd lost Livia, his mate.

Oh, he'd fucked plenty, but that was to escape. Because even after all these centuries, he still craved what he'd lost when she'd been ripped from him.

They'd been bonded, and never once had he believed that he would ever feel that same emotional connection with another female.

And yet this woman—Sinclair's daughter—not only caught his attention, but sparked his awareness.

The intensity of his reaction to Callie had taken him by surprise, and he told himself that he was simply attracted to her beauty. That he just wanted to fuck her—but that wasn't true at all.

He wanted to protect her.

He wanted to have her.

Dammit, he may not have met her before tonight, but he *knew* her. Her heart. Her core.

And that's why he stood there in the dark.

That's why he was watching her door.

And that's why the moment she left the building, he was going to follow her—all the way to wherever the hell that might lead.

* * * *

"Callie, I didn't realize you'd come in. Why on earth are you sitting in the dark?"

I look over at Nurse Bennett and shrug, feeling small and a bit lost. "I just wanted to be here."

"You okay, honey?"

I'm curled up under a thin blanket on the lumpy couch in my father's private hospital room. She sits down beside me and puts her hand on my knee. I expect her to say comforting things. Like how just because the doctors are already talking about transferring him to a nursing home doesn't mean that he might not still pull through.

She doesn't say that, though, and I'm grateful, because I know she doesn't believe it. The truth is, despite what I told Raine, I don't think my dad's going to get better, and I hate myself for that.

"Still nothing today?" I ask, though the question is just for form. Since the stroke, he's spoken only once, and that was to the EMS tech who came after a pedestrian found him sprawled on the street in front of his shop.

"I'm sorry, honey."

"What do you think he was trying to say?" I hate how needy I sound, but I can't help but cling to those last words, as if they were a message for me that, if I only understood, would somehow change everything.

"Don't do that to yourself, Callie. We've talked about this. A stroke is a traumatic event to the brain, and your father didn't just have one stroke but several in quick succession. In that situation, hallucinations are common."

"A pillar of fire with the face of a man? That's common?"

"That's why they call it a hallucination."

"But why that?"

She squeezes my hand. "There's probably no reason at all. You can twist yourself up trying to find meaning where there's none to be found."

I nod because I know she's right. "I'm going to miss you."

"I'm going to miss both of you. Have you decided what you're going to do long term?"

I draw a deep breath. The decision I've made is so permanent, and I hate that I'm making it for my dad, too. But the days keep moving forward, and I have to move with them.

"I talked with a nursing home in Texas. I'm going to stay in New York another week and get his shop closed up and hire an agent to sell the property and talk to Sotheby's about putting some of the more important pieces up for auction. Then I'm going to go home, and I'll arrange for Dad's transport to Dallas as soon as a private room opens up. They don't think it'll take too long."

"Well, like I said, I'll miss you both. But it's good that you're going back to your friends and your work, and that you'll have your dad nearby."

I nod and smile, but the truth is that I'm not sure that anywhere will feel like home anymore. Because right now, all I feel is alone.

Nurse Bennett gives my shoulder a friendly pat as she stands. "I'm going to check his vitals and get out of your hair. Don't stay here tonight, sweetie. You should go home where you can get a good night's sleep."

"I will," I say, though that's probably a lie. More nights than not, I fall asleep on this couch. It's strange, I know, but there's something comforting about the buzz and chirp of the machinery. Even the steady rhythm of the air flowing through the oxygen mask gives me some hope. Because as long as these machines are running, my father is alive. And as long as he's alive, he might return to me.

"*I'm trying, sweetheart. You know that I'm trying.*"

"*Daddy?*" I search, but I see nothing but the dark.

"*I'm right here, baby. But I have to tell you—you have to know.*"

"*Have to know what?*"

A low rumbling fills my ears, and I strain to make out words. Nothing is clear, though. Nothing until I hear my father's voice saying, "And you have to be careful."

"*I don't understand.*" *There's a frantic edge to my voice.* "*Daddy, I couldn't hear you. I don't know what you're talking about.*"

"*Look down.*"

I do, and now I can see my hand in his. He squeezes and fire rises up, flames licking our joined hands.

I yank mine free and leap to my feet.

"Daddy!" The word jerks me from sleep, and I realize that I am on my feet and breathing hard. Even now, I can feel the warmth of the flames and the pressure of my father's hand against my own. But there is nothing there, and my father is all the way across the room, still in the bed and attached to the IVs and machines that beep and hum.

I don't remember falling asleep, but I must have, because clearly I have been dreaming.

I close my eyes and press my fingers to my temples. *A nightmare.* Just a nightmare. Not a message. Not a code. Not a portent.

My father had a stroke, and no matter what I may wish or hope or want to be true, I have to suck it up and deal with that.

I think about what Nurse Bennett said, and I know that she is right. I need to get out of here, at least for a while. Bad sleep and nightmares aren't going to help my dad, they aren't going to help me, and they sure as hell aren't going to heal my grief.

At my dad's bedside, I lean over and kiss his cheek. "You be good, Daddy," I whisper. "I'll see you tomorrow."

I'm doing the right thing—I know that. But once I am outside, the idea of going back to the apartment above my father's store doesn't appeal.

I don't want to be alone, and I consider finding a club. Someplace loud enough that I don't have to talk, and with the kind of heavy bass that pounds through you, almost like sex. A place with no cover for women, and enough good-looking guys to make it worth the bother.

I consider it, but I don't do it. That's not what I crave tonight. I don't want to search for something that I know I'm not going to find. I don't want to pretend that being in the arms of some stranger is going to make a difference.

I don't want fake.

And I have no idea how to find something—or someone—who is real.

So I simply wander, walking from the hospital back toward my dad's store on 59th. I don't have a plan, I don't have a purpose, and it isn't until I turn into a small bar with dark wood and dim lights that I realize I want a drink. Maybe even two.

Hell, maybe I'll have three and ease myself into a dreamless sleep.

It's late on a weeknight, and the place isn't crowded. I take one of the empty stools a few seats down from a couple who are clearly on their first date, then settle in.

"By yourself tonight?" the bartender asks as she puts a dish of spicy nuts and pretzels in front of me.

"Sad but true."

"The hell with that," she says. "Sometimes alone is the best way to be. What can I get for you?"

"Sounds like you've been there, done that," I say after I order a glass of Glenmorangie, neat. I'm leaning forward, my elbows on the bar as she pours, then pushes it in front of me.

"Honey, if you knew my ex, you'd understand that I speak only the truth. Trust me. Ginger knows what Ginger knows, and Ginger knows that alone can be just fine and dandy. Especially if you have a battery operated friend."

I bark out a laugh, almost spitting out my first sip of scotch as I do. "I'll keep that in mind."

I wait until she's walked away to check on other customers before taking another sip. It's excellent, and I lean against the back of the stool and relax, thinking that this is exactly what I need. A good drink. A laid-back atmosphere. And a bartender who reminds me of my paralegal back in Dallas, a wild redhead who's never met a stranger and manages to brighten even the crappiest of days. And when you prosecute homicides and sex offenders, some of those days really can be crappy.

I finish my scotch as I check my phone. My boss has a daughter about my age, and he promised to keep work out of my inbox except in the direst of emergencies. If the state of my e-mail is any indication, the criminal underworld in Texas hasn't completely exploded, for which I'm grateful.

At the same time, I'm feeling a little irrelevant. I can't help my dad and my job is sailing smoothly without me. I couldn't even help Rainer Engel, and now he's probably never going to get his amulet, because I have no idea what it looks like or where it might be. And none of the recent purchase orders and invoices I've reviewed in the store suggest that my father had acquired the thing at all, despite Raine's certainty that Daddy had not only acquired it, but was expecting Raine to come by and get it.

I trace my finger over the rim of my glass as I think about Raine.

You want something real? He's about as real as it gets.

The thought comes unbidden into my mind, and I have a hard time dismissing it, as much as I try.

I don't want to think about Rainer Engel. Not like that. I don't want to remember his mouth on mine. I don't want to think about his hands on my skin. I don't want to remember the way my body fired merely from his proximity or the way his touch had both consumed and overwhelmed me.

He was larger than life, commanding without being overpowering, and his kiss had completely filled my senses, making me feel more alive than I'd felt in a very long time.

I don't want to think of any of that, and yet what choice do I have? Because now that he is in my thoughts, he has possessed me completely, his memory alone as commanding as the man himself, and now I'm feeling antsy and wild and I just want to be home alone in the dark with these wild thoughts and decadent memories.

I toss a twenty onto the bar and stand up. Then I turn—and then I gasp.

Raine.

He's right there, just inches away, and there is a hunger on his face so potent I have to reach for the bar to steady myself.

"With me, angel."

"Excuse me?" My pulse beats in my ear, so loud that it has drowned out everything except the two of us and the sound of my own breathing.

"You heard me." He moves closer, then reaches for the bar as well. The result is that I'm trapped, with a barstool on one side of me, the bar itself on the other, and Raine in front of me. Between us, the air crackles and pops, alive with the heat we are generating. "You're coming with me."

I open my mouth to protest, but find myself asking, "Where?"

It's a tactical error on my part, and one that isn't lost on the man. His smile flows like liquid sin, and instead of answering, he simply holds out his hand.

"This guy bothering you?" Ginger stands like a pit bull behind the bar, and I can't help but smile at the thought of her going up against the likes of Raine.

Raine's body doesn't shift but I see the storm building in those exceptional blue eyes. "How about it, angel? Am I bothering you?"

I'm bothered, all right. But not in the way Ginger means. Slowly, I shake my head. Even more slowly, I reach for his hand. "It's okay," I say, surprised that there is no hesitation in my voice. "I'm with him."

His fingers twine with mine, and as before, I feel that shock of connection, only this time it seems even more potent, as if this contact is a key, and by merely taking his hand I have opened a door that I may never be able to close.

Chapter 3

Raine held tight to her hand, reveling in the sensation of her skin against his. Of the familiarity of this woman he had only just met—and yet he was becoming increasingly certain that he already knew her deeply. Intimately.

He needed to feel her—to touch her. He needed to bury himself in her and find out if what he believed was true. If Callie Sinclair was truly the miracle he suspected.

Desire and need welled up in him, and he pulled her close, pressing his other hand to the small of her back. He searched her eyes, shining now with emerald fire, and was relieved to see no fear, no hesitation. And yet the worry that he'd seen on her face as she'd left the hospital still lingered, and he was overwhelmed by a wave of fierce protectiveness.

Had he thought he needed her in his bed to satisfy his own craving? He did, yes, but that was no longer his primary desire. On the contrary, he wanted, *needed*, to erase her worry. To ease her. To hold her as she opened up, both wanting him and trusting him.

He needed to build—or rebuild—this connection between them. Because it wasn't just her body he intended to claim, it was the woman—body, mind, soul.

He released her back, surrendering to the urge to brush his fingertips over her cheek. As he did, she closed her eyes, and her soft sigh of pleasure was like ambrosia to him.

"You've had a rough day."

Her eyes fluttered open. "You've been following me." There was no accusation in her voice. She was simply stating a fact.

"Yes."

She tilted her head, as if surprised by his ready admission. "This isn't about the amulet, is it?"

"No, Callie. It's not."

She licked her lips, and he could see the confusion wisp across her features. Confusion, yes. But something more, too. Hope? Recognition?

He shook himself, afraid that all he was seeing on her was the reflection of his own hope and desire.

He smiled to set her at ease. "Is that a problem?"

"No."

The immediacy of her answer bolstered him, and he felt a tightening in his groin. He wanted to hold her close, to feel the press of her body against his and let the thrum of her heartbeat mix with his own.

"It's just—" She gently withdrew her hand from his, and it seemed to him as if she'd ripped the fabric of the world out from under him. "I—I don't usually—"

"What?"

She shook her head as if banishing her thoughts even as a hint of a smile tugged at her lips. "If it's not the amulet, what is it you want from me?"

Christ, what a question. "So many things," he finally said, because that was the best truth that he knew. "Right now, I want to soothe you."

"Oh."

Her voice trembled slightly, and he tightened his fingers into a fist, fighting the urge to touch her. There was a storm building between them, making the air crackle and burn, that spark or connection or whatever it was vibrating in the damp night air. If he reached out—if he let skin touch skin—he knew with unerring certainty that she would come with him, submit to him.

And though he wanted that—dear lord, how he wanted that— he wanted more to have the choice be entirely hers. To come not because she was reacting to the heat, but to him. Not following that thread of connection, but following her heart.

He watched, holding his own breath even as she drew in hers. "What does that mean?" she asked. "When you say you want to soothe me?"

"That depends on you, angel. Do you want me to take you back to your father's house and see you safely tucked away for the night?"

He saw the small frown curve at her mouth and felt a ping of joy that the thought of simply escorting her home did not satisfy her.

"Or do you need something different?"

He could see by the fire in her eyes that she did, and he pressed on, rightly or wrongly using words in the same way that he wanted to use his hands. To caress and tease and pleasure. To bring her close. To make her his.

"Do you need to forget? To get lost in the feel of my hands upon your skin, my mouth on your breast? Do you want to lose yourself in passion, in submission, in pleasure?"

He could see the effect that his words had on her. The flush on her skin. The parting of her lips. The way she moved a hairsbreadth closer to him.

He saw—and he was satisfied.

"I'll give you what you need, angel, I promise you that. But not until you tell me what that is."

"I don't know what I need," she whispered, her head tilted down. "I only know what I want." She lifted her face to his, her eyes burning, and the words she spoke held enough power to bring him to his knees. "Please, Raine. Right now, all I want is you."

****

All I want is you.

The sound of my voice hasn't faded when his hand twines in my hair and his arm goes around my waist.

In one wild, violent motion, he pulls me hard against him. I gasp, both in surprise and pleasure, as my breasts press against his chest. As my hips grind against his.

We are well matched in height, and I can feel the hot demand of his erection against my belly, and when he slants his mouth over mine, I cannot help my moan of pleasure from this sensual assault.

He takes advantage of the sound, using his tongue to tease my mouth open. It takes little effort—I want this, after all. Want his hands, hot and wild upon me. Want his mouth all over me.

And god help me, I want his cock inside me.

The thought shocks me out of myself, and I pull back, breathing hard. "We're on the street."

The grin he flashes is decidedly wicked. "Is that a problem?" There's no denying the tease in his voice, and I don't fight the smile that tugs at my mouth.

"I don't do exhibitionism."

"No?" He looks me up and down so slowly and intimately that it feels as though he is making a liar out of me right there by burning off every stitch of clothes simply with the heat of his gaze. "Then tell me, Callie. What do you do?"

I lick my lips, undone by the sensual images his four little words have conjured in my mind. I have no hope of a comeback. I have completely surrendered. "I—"

But his finger upon my lip silences me. "No. Don't tell me. I'd rather find out myself."

He traces his fingertip gently along my lower lip, leaving my mouth feeling warm and swollen, as if I've been very well kissed.

It is as if he has flipped a switch in me, making me aware of my entire body. From this sensual tingle in my lips, to the tightness in my breasts, to the tiny beads of sweat that have popped up at the nape of my neck. And let's not forget the way my sex clenches in both demand and anticipation of his touch.

In other words, he's made me a wreck, and right then if he repeated his question, I'd have to tell him that I'd do pretty much anything.

We are still on the street right outside the bar, and as my senses return, I notice that we have actually drawn a small audience. Despite what movies might suggest, the kind of wild kisses that mimic fucking are not par for the course on the sidewalks of the Upper East Side. I notice an elderly couple, the man looking at us over the top of his glasses with what looks to me like lecherous interest. I clutch Raine's arm. "If you want this to go anywhere at all, then get me out of here now."

"As you wish," he says, then nods toward the street where a sleek black limo has just pulled up.

I hesitate because it takes a moment for me to register that the limo and Raine are a set.

"You look surprised," Raine says as the driver opens the door for us. I cast a glance between him and the interior. His rough, rebellious looks and sleeves of tats might seem in stark contrast to the pristine leather interior that suggests boardrooms and opera rather than beer and heavy metal. But that isn't what Raine is about, and I already knew that. He has too much control, too much self-possession. A limo suits him just fine.

But I have a feeling he keeps a bike for fun.

"No," I say as I step inside. "I'm really not. I was just thinking that I was relieved you didn't bring your Harley. I'm not in the mood to ride shotgun."

He sits beside me on the leather bench at the back of the limo. There is a bar along the sidewall, and he turns to it, then casually pours a glass of scotch on the rocks. "Actually, it's a Macchia Nera."

I gape at him. "Seriously?"

The fact that I have a clue what he's talking about obviously surprises him. "You've heard of it?"

I take the scotch he hands me, then nod. "My boss is into bikes. That bike is his personal nirvana. He once told me he could either buy the Macchia Nera or a house. When he factored in his wife and kids, he went with the house, but for a while there it was close."

"Fortunately not a dilemma I've faced."

"You'd choose the bike?"

"It would be hard to be homeless. No roof as with a car. But she's a sweet bike. It might just be worth it. Then again," he added, aiming the full force of those brilliant blue eyes my direction, "a man will do most anything to take care of the woman he loves. I imagine that your boss didn't even consider the loss of his bike a sacrifice."

I shift a bit in the seat, then take a sip of the scotch. It's good. Exceptionally good, actually, and I tell him so. "Most men would have offered me wine."

"I'm not most men."

"Yeah. I actually figured that out."

"Clever girl."

I smile at him, enjoying talking to him even more than I like looking at him. But right then, I'm not interested in talking. Or in looking for that matter. All I want to do is feel.

I move to set the scotch aside, but he takes the glass from my hand, then slips his finger into the liquid and slides the digit into his own mouth. My body clenches merely from the sight, and my lips tingle with awareness. "Raine."

He shakes his head, then withdraws his finger and holds it over his lips in a gesture of silence. Then he dips into the scotch again, this time painting my lips with his fingertip.

I almost melt from the contact, and when my lips part on a gentle sigh, he eases his finger into my mouth. I take it greedily, relishing the taste of his skin mingled with the scotch. I draw his finger in, sucking and teasing him with my tongue, and it is easy enough to see the effect that I am having on him reflected on his face.

I meet his eyes, and when I do, the entire world fades away. There is only the two of us, and passion, and need.

I draw him in deeper. I'm greedy now, wanting more. Wanting everything. And so help me, I want to make him come. I want to see this strong, magnificent man lose himself in wild abandon—and I want to know that I was the one who took him there.

Shamelessly, I ease forward, my fingers groping for the fly on his jeans, but he gently shakes his head even as he takes my hand and presses it over the steel-hard length of his erection. "I can't tell you how much I want those lips around my cock," he says as he withdraws his finger. "But not just yet."

I swallow as he takes my hand from him and lifts it to his mouth. He kisses my palm, then repeats the kiss on my other hand. "Sit back," he orders, even as he shifts to face me better. "Eyes closed."

"I want to see you."

"And I want you to feel. Close your eyes, Callie."

There is no room for argument in his voice, and my willingness to comply surprises me, as I do not usually give in so easily to a man's demand.

Raine, however, is no ordinary man, and he is proving that point even now as he sets my entire body on fire merely by the gentle stroke of his finger along my collar. His finger is damp, and I can hear the tingle of ice as he once more dips his finger into the scotch and then uses that digit to paint my flesh. Then I feel his mouth on me, tracing my jawline, trailing down my neck. His lips tease me. His tongue tastes me. And soon enough his fingers descend to the open collar of my shirt.

I'm wearing a blue linen button-down, and as his fingers flick each button open, I know that he is revealing the innocent pale pink bra, though I am feeling very far from innocent at the moment.

He finishes the buttons and spreads the shirt open. I can't help it, and I open my eyes to see that he is gazing upon me as if I am something holy. "You're stunning," he says, and I feel my cheeks heat with the words. "And you broke the rules. Eyes closed, Callie."

I draw in a breath, but comply. Immediately, I feel his fingertip, again wet with scotch, tracing from cleavage to navel. "I think this is my favorite way to enjoy my favorite drink," he says, making me giggle. But my laughter stops when he drips more scotch into my navel, then proceeds to lap it up, his tongue working such magic on me that the muscles in my abdomen quiver with need and I arch my back in a desperate attempt for just a little more contact, a little more connection.

Then his nimble fingers unbutton my jeans and ease down my zipper. I'm wearing thong panties, and he trails his fingertip along my pubic bone, just at the top of the material. Then it is not his fingertip that I feel, but his lips, and my sex clenches with such intense need that I know I am desperately, hopelessly wet.

I want him to take me further, and I bite my lower lip in anticipation of where he will go next. Tongue or finger sliding under the waistband. Easing my jeans down. Teasing my clit with soft kisses. Fucking me hard with his tongue.

My body trembles merely from the anticipation, and there is no denying that he has brought me close, so very close, and I am primed and ready for his next touch.

Except it doesn't come.

In fact, he leaves me entirely.

I open my eyes, confused, to find him no longer sitting beside me, but on the bench seat exactly opposite me. He is sitting up, his legs apart, and there is no mistaking either the bulge of his erection or the heat in his eyes.

"What are you—"

"Take off your clothes."

"What?"

His gaze skims over me, and there is such a feral hunger in his eyes that I swear I almost come right then. "You heard me. I want you naked."

I start to shake my head, but he simply holds up a finger again.

"I want to see you, Callie. I want to see the glow of arousal on your skin. I want to get hard while you touch yourself. I want to bring you to heights of pleasure you haven't even imagined, and I want to hold you while you scream my name and cry out in release."

I am breathing hard, and there is no hiding how fiercely turned on I am.

"You say you aren't into exhibitionism? I'm going to make it my mission to change your mind. So take off your clothes, Callie, or everything stops and I'll drive you home. The choice is yours. But I will tell you that I desperately hope that you do as I say because the night is young, and this is only the beginning."

Chapter 4

Take off your clothes.

His words flow through me, both dangerous and enticing.

Part of me wants to tell him to go to hell, but the bigger part wants to strip bare and get myself off, tormenting him by not allowing him to touch me.

I want to feel this—want to feel wild. Out of control.

I want to take it as far as it can go—but only with Raine.

Across from me, he still sits, silently watching me, his erection so tight I'm surprised he doesn't burst through his jeans.

Slowly, I slip off the shirt, then toss it to the side, leaving me clad in only my bra, jeans, and wedge sandals.

I reach behind me and unfasten my bra, then shimmy it off and drop it on top of my shirt. And then—because I want to run this show at least a little—I cup my own breasts, then pinch my own nipples, gratified at the sound of pleasure he makes. Even more gratified when he puts his hand on his cock and strokes himself through his jeans.

"The rest," he says, and I revel in pure feminine satisfaction when I hear the strain in his voice.

I comply willingly, maybe even too eagerly. I want to be free of my clothes. I want the pleasure of feeling his eyes upon me and knowing that my body excites him.

But I also want this to be a show, a seduction. I have no illusions about who is in charge here, but I do want to keep a tiny bit of the power to tease and entice.

With that in mind, I slide my hand down over my belly to my jeans. Since he's already very considerately unbuttoned them for me, I only have to lift my hips to shimmy out of them. I do that, moving slowly as I free myself from jeans and shoes.

"You're stunning."

My cheeks warm with pleasure, and I continue this erotic dance, sliding my finger down into my panties and finding my clit, throbbing with a demand for attention.

"Take them off." His voice is clear and authoritative, and just the sound of it—of his command—heightens my arousal. "Then spread your legs and tease yourself."

I do, not the least bit shy. On the contrary, I want this. Everything he has to give and more. And so I do as he says, following his bold words as he tells me to stroke my inner thigh, to tease my clit, to thrust three fingers deep into my cunt.

"Do you like that?" he asks, and I can only moan in assent. "Does it get you off knowing that I'm watching you? That I'm imagining my cock deep inside you? Can you imagine it, Callie? Can you feel me fucking you hard?"

"Yes." It is all I can do to get the word out. I am soaked. My body clenching around my fingers, my clit swollen and demanding. And through all of it, I know that he has his eyes on me. That my show is turning him on, too, and that he is painfully aware of just how much I want him.

"Is it enough?" he asks. "Your hands? Your fingers?"

"No."

"Tell me what you want, angel."

"You. Please. God, Raine. Please."

"Come here."

I practically leap to the other side of the limo even as he rids himself of shoes and jeans and briefs. He still wears that T-shirt, and I remedy that quickly by taking hold of the hem and pulling it over his head to fully reveal his hard, taut body, which is covered in tats. In fact, almost every inch of the man that I can see except his magnificent cock and his face is decorated in wings and talons and the proud faces and beaks of birds that I can only assume are phoenixes, especially with the hint of flames lapping at them.

It's not a look I usually go for, but on Raine it seems to fit. As if it's not decoration, but part of who he is. I don't understand it, and right then, I don't care. I just want to feel him inside me. I want it wild. I want it hot.

Without asking or being told, I climb onto the seat and straddle him.

"That's a girl," he says in approval.

"Condom?" I'm on the pill, but pregnancy's not the only thing a girl has to be careful about.

"I don't have one. But I swear I'm clean. Do you trust me?"

I hesitate, because I have my rules. But so help me, I do trust him. Me, who so rarely trusts any man.

I nod, and I see the fire in his eyes. "Now show me. Show me what it is you want."

I can wait no longer. I lean forward, one hand twining in his hair and holding him steady as I close my mouth over his and capture him in a deep, wet kiss. I slide my other hand down my body, sending an electric shimmer running through me when I graze the pad of my thumb over my clit.

I find his cock, hard and thick and velvety smooth, between our bodies. He's rigid, and I have to rise up on my knees to position him, but when I feel the head of his cock at my core, the sensation is almost enough to make me lose my mind.

I'm desperately wet, and I tease both of us for a bit before lowering myself onto him. But it isn't enough for him, and his hands are at my hips and he's thrusting me down, impaling me hard upon him. I cry out, not from pain, but from the glorious sensation of being completely taken. Utterly fucked.

"Christ, you feel good."

I say nothing. At the moment, I'm really not capable of forming words.

His mouth closes over my breast, and I suck in air sharply at the overwhelming sensation of his mouth sucking hard on my nipple even while he pistons me so wildly. I press my palms to his shoulders, wanting leverage, and bring myself down even harder, faster. I am craving him like a woman starved, and in that moment, I cannot imagine not being connected like this. Not feeling him inside me. Not riding him hard.

"I want to do everything to you." He lifts his head from my breast and tilts up to look at me. His eyes burn like blue flame, and I feel like I could fall inside them. "There is nothing I won't give you. Nowhere I won't take you to give you pleasure."

He kisses me, long and deep, then slides his finger into my mouth. I suck it hard, and with each tug I feel the corresponding pull in my sex and the tightening of my muscles around his cock.

But that is not what he wants, and even as he tongues my mouth, he slides his hand around to tease my ass with his now-damp finger. I cry out in surprise at the intimate contact. I've never gone there—never wanted to with anyone else. And yet I want it with Raine. I want him to fill me completely, and I feel as though there is nothing he can do—no way that he can touch me that I would deny him.

"Touch yourself," he whispers. "Tease your clit. I want to feel the storm building inside you."

That is something else I've never done with other men. Oh, sure, I've gotten myself off after I sent them running, if they failed to take me all the way. But with them watching? That wasn't something I wanted to share.

Now, though, I do not hesitate. As I had done for show earlier, I slide my hand down and finger my clit, using long strokes so that I can not only tease myself, but so that I can feel the slick heat of his cock as he moves in and out of me.

I am lost in a sensual feast. His cock deep inside me. His finger teasing my ass. His mouth on my breast, and my own hand playing with my clit. My legs are wide, and I am riding him hard, and he is thrusting so deep inside me that it feels as though he is completely filling me.

"You're mine." He growls out the words, his mouth capturing mine before releasing it just enough to speak, the words so close that it feels almost as though I'm saying them. "Come with me now," he says, even as he releases into me, his body thrusting violently and heightening my own pleasure.

"Come for me," he growls again. "And come back to me…"

Even as he makes the demand, he thrusts his finger inside me and impales me hard on his cock so that I am utterly and completely filled. And as if I am bound to obey this man, my body soars upward, then shatters into a million pieces that seem to dance and swirl and mesh with Raine, who is spinning up in the heavens with me.

It is wild and wicked and wonderful, and then slowly, so very slowly, I begin to reassemble in his arms.

"Mmm," I murmur, certain I must be the most thoroughly fucked woman on the planet. *"La petite mort."*

"Why do you say that?"

"That's what the French call an orgasm. The little death. As wonderfully destroyed as I feel right now, I think it's accurate."

He chuckles, then shifts me so that I am more comfortably on his lap. I trace my fingers over his tattoos. "I like them," I say. "They suit you."

"Do they?"

I hear humor in his voice that I don't understand. "What's funny?"

"You're more intuitive than you realize. Those tats are my little deaths."

I frown, completely confused. "What do you mean?"

"It doesn't matter. Right now I don't want to talk. I only want to hold you."

As if in contradiction to his own statement, he presses the button for the intercom. "Dennis," he says. "Take us to Number 36."

He releases the button without receiving a reply, then turns to me. "My home."

I nod, but even as I do, I feel something cold twisting inside me, as if it is determined to push away everything wonderful that I've just felt with this man.

I let him hold me, and in his arms I feel warm and safe. It scares me, in fact, how comfortable I feel with Raine because I have never felt this way before. I'm self-aware enough to know that I sleep with men to fill a hole, but it just seems to get deeper every day. And the truth is, I never walk into sex expecting anything but the physical exhaustion that can take me out of myself.

I certainly never expect a connection. Never expect to fill that hole, even if just a little.

And yet with Raine...

I shift in his arms and sit up.

"Cold?"

"A bit," I lie as I reach for my bra and put it on, then follow with my panties and jeans. He is still naked, as stunningly beautiful as a vengeful god with his marked skin wild against the black backdrop of leather. And even though I am sated, my body responds, even as my mind starts to pull back.

"Is this what you don't usually do? Go home with men you've just met?"

I smirk. "No. I do that more often than I should." My admission surprises me, and I glance at him, but he doesn't seem shocked, just curious.

"Then what did you mean earlier? When you said you don't usually...what?"

I don't usually have expectations other than sex. I don't usually feel anything before being with a man.

I almost tell him that, and I have to cut off my words before I reveal too much of this emotional stew that is filling me.

I tell myself I don't want to go there; I don't want to feel a connection I don't understand.

I am, of course, lying. There's little I want more. Isn't that what I keep telling Kelly? That I feel there's someone out there. Someone who fits me?

And doesn't she keep telling me that I have to open myself up? That burning through men like a book of matches is a bad idea? That I don't have to project my mother's abandonment on every potential relationship.

I know that she is right. I even know what I want.

And yet I also know that the possibility that I may have found it in this man is terrifying.

What if I'm wrong? What if I expose too much of myself? What if I get too close and just get burned?

"Callie? What is it? What did you mean?"

"Just—nothing. I just ramble when I'm nervous."

"Do I make you nervous?"

I pull my still-bare feet up onto the seat and look at him, strong and powerful and entirely in control. "Honestly? Yes."

He reaches for his shirt and shrugs it on, apparently realizing that I've moved into the land of serious conversation. "Why?"

"I—I'm sorry. This is—This is bigger than I expected." I lick my lips, looking with mild panic at the brownstones rising up alongside the limo as it slows to a stop. "It doesn't just scare me. It terrifies me. I'm sorry, but I need to go home."

"Stay." The command in his tone is unmistakable. "I told you, all I want to do is soothe you."

I am tempted. So very tempted. But I shake my head. "This has been amazing. Beyond amazing. But I can't stay with you tonight." I need to get clear so that I can think. Because the one thing I definitely can't do around this man is conjure a cohesive thought.

His hand closes over my wrist, and as I melt just a bit from the contact, I can only wish that his touch didn't have such sensual power over me. "I told you, Callie. I'm never leaving you again."

The words resonate through me, as if touching some deep core, but I force myself to shake my head because I need to run. "I don't know what that means, but it doesn't matter. Because you're not leaving me, Raine." Gently, I pull my arm free. "I'm sorry. But right now, I'm the one leaving you."

Chapter 5

I stand on the street, breathing hard, my thoughts spinning.

My entire adult life I've been looking for something. And for the first time, it feels like maybe I found it.

So what the fuck am I doing running away?

"You crave intimacy, Callie. And yet you run from it." Kelly's words seem to fill my head, and though I try to shut her out, she just keeps on talking. *"Perhaps it stems from the loss of your mother when you were so young, perhaps something else. But until you understand why you're afraid of getting close, you're never going to have a fulfilling relationship. And you are too extraordinary a woman not to open yourself up to love and friendship."*

She's right. I know she's right. And I take a single step back toward the limo. It's still curbside, the door still open. I cannot see through the tinted glass. I have no way of knowing if he is watching me, and yet I am certain that he is. Watching, but not coming after me, and I am grateful for that small mercy because I have to decide this for myself, and I fear that if he steps out of that limo and holds out his hand to me, that I will rush into his arms and let him take me inside Number 36.

I want that—so help me, I want it so badly I can imagine how it feels. The sensation of my feet flying over pavement to meet him. The impact of my body against his as his arms close around me. The hard demand of his mouth against mine.

And yet there's something else, too. *Fear.*

Kelly would tell me to examine that fear and push past it, but as a therapist, that's her job. As an assistant district attorney, I know that isn't always the best thing to do. Sometimes fear is a good thing. Sometimes fear tells you to run, to save your own life.

Ignore that instinct and you do so at your own peril.

I've seen it time and time again on the faces of too many victims. In the photographs of too many corpses.

I do not believe that Raine would hurt me physically, but I am desperately afraid that the intensity of my desire for him isn't real. That this connection I feel with him is nothing more than an illusion, because how can it be real? How can someone I've known for less than a day have seeped so far under my skin when no one else in my entire life has been able to do that?

The world is already taking my father from me, and I don't think I can stand the pain of being wrong about Raine. Of getting close and losing him, too.

And somehow, I am certain that I *will* lose him. That he will draw me close, and then let me go.

No, that's not entirely true. What I'm certain of is that he already *has* let me go.

I frown because I know the thought makes no sense—I just met the man, and I know damn well he would welcome me into his arms. And yet I cannot shake this certainty. This feeling.

This…memory?

I roll my eyes at the thought. Clearly, the night has rattled me more than I realized. Which is all the more reason to just walk away.

Better to hold tight to the passion and joy I felt in Raine's arms. Better to cherish it like something wild and precious and fragile, and to pull it out for comfort when I feel lost and alone.

Better all that than to open the door to pain and fear and heartbreak.

And so I make the only decision I can.

I turn away from the limo, and I walk away, heading toward Madison, where I can turn and continue toward 59th Street and home.

* * * *

Raine fought back the rising sense of desolation.

She'd left him.

The thought was…well, it was unthinkable. After all this time to have found her again—and, yes, he was certain that he'd found her—only to watch her walk away.

He wanted to run after her, but he quelled the urge. He knew her. He'd recognized her essence the first moment he saw her, and when he had entered her—when she had exploded in passion in his arms—the last of his doubts were swept away. But he understood that the same was not true for Callie.

She had felt a pull, of that much he was certain. But she didn't know the origin of it. And the intensity of the connection scared her.

He may not like that simple fact, but he could understand it. And he could give her time.

She would come back to him—or he would go to her.

Either way, he could be patient.

He'd been alone for three thousand years, thinking her lost to him forever, believing he was condemned to an eternity alone. He could wait a little while longer while he decided what to do.

Not too long, however, as he still had to find the amulet. And to do that, he might have to press Callie before she was ready. Unless, of course, he could find another way.

He considered his options as he looked out the window toward Number 36. The five-story brownstone had been owned by the brotherhood since the late eighteen hundreds, when it had been acquired after the first occupant died in an ill-conceived duel and the property was put on the market to settle his considerable debts.

The first and second floors housed a gentleman's club, Dark Pleasures, which Mal had established in 1895 despite some in the brotherhood's protests. But Mal had been insistent, and one did not cross Mal, especially not after an encounter with Christina, when the rage and regret flowed through him.

And ultimately, all of the brotherhood had to agree that the club served a valuable purpose. There was no denying the usefulness of a central meeting place. A place to talk. To bring potential resources and informants.

And, most important, to be themselves.

Though the club did have mortal members and staff, the brotherhood was selective. And no one but the brotherhood was permitted in the VIP room.

That was where Raine intended to go now. Though part of him wanted nothing more than to retire to his apartment on the top floor of Number 36, he had a duty to discuss the amulet with Liam and Mal, his superiors. And he had the need to discuss Callie with his friends.

* * * *

"Checkmate." Malcolm leaned back in the plush leather armchair, then took a puff from the cigar he held. Across the table from him, Dante frowned as he studied the chessboard. Then he blew out a breath, took a long sip of scotch, and used his thumb and forefinger to topple his king.

"Son-of-a-bitch."

"You should know better than to challenge Mal," Raine said as he approached and took a seat in one of the two empty chairs that surrounded the table on which the chessboard stood.

"What can I say?" Dante replied. "I'm an eternal optimist."

"I think 'fool' is the word you're looking for." Mal's grin was smug and cool, just like the man himself. He calculated everything, never misstepped, and handled the power and responsibility of being one of the brotherhood's two leaders with unerring precision and devotion. Raine loved all of the brotherhood, but it was to Mal he most often turned. And it was Mal who most understood his pain, since he carried the weight of a similar burden.

"And this is all I have to say to you," Dante retorted, displaying his middle finger.

Mal's lips twitched, and Raine sat back in the chair, glad to be back in New York and among friends.

He glanced over as Jessica approached from across the room, then bent down and pressed a kiss to his forehead before handing him a glass. "Macallan. On the rocks. You look like you could use it."

"Thanks," he said, taking a welcome sip as she sat on the arm of his chair and studied his face. He kept his expression bland. Jessica was a healer—and he knew she was searching for injuries—but she had the ability to see so much more than that.

Across the table, Liam settled into the empty chair, his broad shoulders and well-muscled body filling the seat. He was the second leader of the brotherhood, and no one looking at him would doubt that. There was power and control in every one of his movements, and he had only to enter a room to command it.

Now, his eyes flicked from Jessica to Raine. "Just back from the field, and the first thing you do is flirt with my mate?"

"Not the first thing," Raine corrected easily. "And no. I know better than that." He shot Jessica a wicked grin. "She'd beat the crap out of me."

"She damn sure would," Jessica agreed cheerfully, then squeezed his hand before circling the chairs and settling into Liam's lap. He drew her close, then kissed her passionately, and though Raine was used to the way the two of them couldn't keep their hands off each other, tonight it ate at him. As if their affection was eating a hole through his gut that only Callie could fill.

He forced himself to look away and found Mal's eyes bearing down on him, his expression questioning.

Raine met his glance mildly, not yet willing to give anything away.

After a moment, Mal seemed to relax. He leaned forward and stubbed out his cigar, then returned his attention to Raine. "The mission?"

"A success."

"Kirkov is out of the picture?"

"He's dead." Raine pressed his fingertips to his temples. Not simply because he could so vividly remember the Bulgarian serial killer that Phoenix Security had been hired to locate and terminate, but because he knew where this conversation would inevitably lead.

"And the fuerie?" Mal asked, referring to the malevolent energy that it was the brotherhood's sworn duty to hunt. "Was there time for it to transfer?"

Raine tipped his glass back and finished his scotch. "It's over, Mal. I took Kirkov over the Asparuhov Bridge. He was history at impact, and there was no one around the fuerie could enter." He lifted the glass, remembered he'd already finished it, and silently cursed.

"How much of the fuerie's essence was in the man?" Liam asked as Dante passed Raine his glass. Raine took it gratefully and slammed back the last of his friend's drink.

"Minuscule," Raine reported. "Kirkov was fucked up all on his own. Even so, having the fuerie inside him made it that much worse, and now they're both dead. The human monster, and the sliver of the dark within him."

Raine stood. "So that's it. Mission accomplished." He held up Dante's glass. "I'm going to go get us both a refill."

"Wait." Mal spoke softly but firmly, and though Raine wanted to tell his friend to leave him the fuck alone, that wasn't something that he could tell his leader. "Let me see your back."

"Dammit, Mal—"

"Now."

Raine stiffened, taking the time to pull himself together. He knew the rules, and the biggest was that an agent didn't put himself in a position to be killed.

Fuck.

He stood up and lifted his shirt, revealing the newly extended tail feather of the phoenix that marked his back.

"Goddammit, Raine. Didn't I tell you not to take any chances? And you what? Threw yourself over a fucking bridge?"

"I'm still standing, aren't I? I've still got my humanity, don't I?"

He watched as Mal's expression hardened and he pointed at Dante and Jessica, both of whom stood and moved to the far side of the room. After a moment, Liam left as well. Which meant this was going to be an off-the-record conversation and not an official reprimand.

Frankly, Raine wasn't in the mood for either.

"I'm going to crash," he said. "We can do this in the morning."

He started to walk away, but the pain in his friend's voice drew him back.

"Dammit, Raine. I know you want to punish yourself for losing Livia, but it wasn't your fault. You can't keep going into the burn, because one of these days you're not going to come out of it."

"But I will," he said. "That's what we are now, isn't it? We can't die. We can just be reborn in fire." For millennia, he and the brotherhood had been immortal. Blessed—or cursed—with eternal life, death was not the end. Instead, like a phoenix, they were reborn in fire, and with each rebirth, the tattoo that marked them as a member of the brotherhood grew and changed. Raine, unlike his brethren, was almost fully covered with tats.

"That's bullshit," Mal said. "Die enough and you'll be reborn, but you won't be alive. You'll be a living shell. Your humanity burned out. And as many times as you've pushed—as many times as you've burned—you must be getting close to being hollow. To burning out everything human that lives inside you."

Mal spoke the truth. The brotherhood might have defeated death, but there was a price—burn too many times, and a man's humanity could be burned right out of him, too. It was a not a slow process. Not a gradual descent into the void of madness. Instead, it happened suddenly, with little warning.

It had happened two centuries ago to Samson, the most reckless of the brothers, and now he was nothing more than a cold, conscienceless assassin who lived out his days in the brotherhood's German facility, called into service only in the most dire of circumstances.

"Dammit, Raine," Mal continued. "Do you want to end up like Samson? Do you think Livia would want that? Do you think I could stand it? I already lost one friend that way. Would you really have me lose another?"

Raine closed his eyes, drew a breath, then sat back down. "Honestly, Mal, there was a time I wouldn't have cared. When I welcomed each fight, and the more dangerous the better. When I craved a mortal wound. When I longed for death, because I wanted nothing more than to burn the pain out of me. That's what humanity is, isn't it?" He pressed a hand to his heart. "These bodies that are made to suffer. They are the essence of humanity, aren't they? Love. Tenderness. Pain. The wild storm of emotions, and I wanted to simply end it."

"I know," Mal said simply.

"You must understand that." He looked his friend in the eye, knowing all too well that Mal had suffered loss, too. Perhaps even more keenly than he had. Livia at least, was gone in an instant, or so he'd believed until just a few hours ago. But Mal was tormented over and over by the memory of all he'd had with Christina. And everything that he could never have again.

Raine saw the pain play over Mal's face, and he regretted his words. Still, he needed Mal to understand.

Mal, however, was not taking the bait. "Wanted to," Mal repeated carefully. "You said you *wanted* to simply end it. Past tense. Something has changed, Raine. Tell me what."

Raine ran his hand over his close-cropped hair and tried to figure out where to start. "She's not gone. Mal, I swear to you, I've met her. I've held her."

Mal's eyes narrowed. "What the hell are you talking about?"

"Livia. Her essence."

He saw the pain flash across Mal's face. "We lost Livia, Raine. She was thrust into the void. We both saw it."

"We were wrong. Her essence is here, Mal."

"Raine..."

"*No.* Listen to me. This isn't grief or wishful thinking. It's fact. And Livia's essence remains. It's in Sinclair's daughter."

He watched Mal struggle to keep his expression bland. "The antiques dealer?"

"I went by his store after I returned from Bulgaria. Sinclair had a lead on the seventh amulet—no," he added, before Mal could ask about the amulet, "it didn't pan out. But she was there, Mal." He leaned forward, his elbows on his knees. "Callie Sinclair. It's her."

"You can't be certain. Not yet."

"Yes," Raine said, thinking of the way Callie came in his arms. "I am."

Mal leaned back, his expression making it clear that he realized exactly what Raine meant. That he'd already had this woman in his bed. That they'd reached climax together and in that moment when their energies meshed, he had been certain.

"Well," Mal said. "I always knew you moved fast."

"No jokes," Raine said. "Not about this. Not about her."

Mal studied him, then nodded. "And the girl?"

"She feels it too, Mal."

"She knows? She remembers?"

"No." He shook his head, wishing the answer were otherwise. "Not overtly. But she feels the connection."

"Then why isn't she here?"

His friend was too perceptive by half. "She's human. Such intensity so quickly—it scared her."

Mal nodded. "As you say, she's human. If Livia's essence does live within her, it has mingled with the soul of Callie Sinclair. There is no way to untwine it. They are one. And while Livia may have once been your mate, Callie Sinclair was not."

"I was dead until I found this woman, Mal. And now she fills my heart and my head. I may have only just met her, but I know the core of her. She is the woman for me, Mal. And if she doesn't yet realize that, then I will simply have to spend the rest of my very long life convincing her."

Chapter 6

I walk for an hour, even though the store is only a few minutes away, and end up having to double back. It's worth it, though. I needed to clear my head, and when I finally return to the darkened shop and let myself in, I've convinced myself that walking away was the right thing to do.

I have a job in Texas, after all. A good job that's important and that I love. There's something satisfying about being part of a system that makes sure that evil is punished, and each and every time I get a conviction and some lowlife murderer or rapist gets put behind bars, that hole inside me fills a little.

Maybe I don't have a stellar personal life, but I have my work, and it's valuable and important, and it is not going away.

In the end, the only one you can count on is yourself. Haven't I known that since the day my mother walked away? And isn't that lesson being driven home now that my father is dying and there is nothing, absolutely nothing, that I can do to change that?

I can't deny that I felt a profound connection to Raine, but that's part of the problem. Because if it's tearing me up this much to walk away after one day, how much of a wreck will I be when I lose him after a month? A year?

Stop it.

Christ, I'm acting like a skittish colt.

I force myself to push away thoughts of Raine. It's over. Done. I'm going back to Texas just like I told Nurse Bennett. I'm getting my father transferred there. And I'm shutting the door on the New York chapter of my life.

And the sooner I finish inventorying the shop, the better.

It's late, but I'm spurred to action. I consider going upstairs to the apartment above the store and changing back into my yoga pants, but I'm afraid if I do that I'll just get too comfortable and end up camped out on the couch in front of the television with a glass of wine and a book.

So I stay down here, lost in the memories that this shop sparks. I spent my childhood inside this space. My father bought it before I was born, and when my mother left us when I was four, we moved out of the small apartment the three of us had shared and into the cramped little studio above the shop.

I didn't mind how small it was; I wanted to escape the memories of my mother as much as my father did, and having a tiny space seemed to help, as if it kept all my memories and fears boxed in close to me.

I liked it so much, in fact, that my dad made me a playhouse in a faux window seat. He added a hinge to make it open from the front, and I would crawl into the tiny area, just big enough for a little girl to lay on her stomach with a flashlight and books and stuffed animals. I'd even sleep there sometimes, safe in that hidden space.

Though nights were spent in the study and my playhouse, I whiled away my days in the shop, exploring the shelves and listening to my dad's stories. He never considered himself a store owner but a knight. A man on a quest. "There's something bigger than us out there, Callie my love," he'd tell me. And I would sit enraptured—and I would believe him.

He had a deep love of history, mythology, and folklore, and I used to wander the store, certain that I would find fairies living in jeweled pillboxes or angels dancing in the light split by a prism.

I never did, but to this day I still look, and it makes me sad to think that all of this will be going away.

With a sigh, I sit on a velvet-upholstered settee, then immediately realize my mistake. I'm tired, a fact that has become only too apparent now that I have stopped moving. I need to either go upstairs and go to bed or get to work on the inventory, but as I lay my head on the upholstered high back, the only strength I can muster is barely sufficient to keep my eyes open.

Just a quick nap, I think. Five minutes, then a cup of coffee, and then I'll get to work.

Just five minutes. After all, it's not like I'm asking for all the time in the world.

Aren't you?

Though I look around for the source of the voice, I find no one. But the store seems to glow now, and I realize I must have fallen asleep, and the glow is probably coming from the rising sun.

As for the voice, it must have been someone in a dream, though I don't remember dreaming at all.

I start to swing my legs off the settee, but I realize that something is wrong. I'm not in the shop at all. I'm in the middle of a forest, with tall trees and a tangle of underbrush, and everything is on fire.

Frantic, I turn in a circle, looking for a way out. As I do, I see that there are all sorts of paths, and as far as I can tell, each one leads to safety. But I do not make a move for any of them.

I realize that I'm not searching for an exit, but hiding. And waiting, though I am not sure what I am waiting for.

But no one comes, and so I stay hidden in the fire, burning and burning until I am raw and scared and tired and alone and—

Suddenly my ears ring with the clanging of bells, as if I'm surrounded by a ring of old-fashioned fire trucks.

I look out toward the flames, and now I see a face.

Raine.

Relief and joy washes over me. *He came.*

I knew he would come, and he did. How could I have doubted, even for a moment?

And yet when he reaches for me through the flames, I am jolted awake by my phone.

"Find the book."

"Daddy?"

"Find the book, find the path. Look to yourself for the answer, and you will find it hidden in plain sight."

"Daddy? Wait. How are you calling me? What are you—"

I jerk upright and realize that I am holding my hand to my ear. My phone is still on the table in front of me.

I've been dreaming.

With a sigh, I rub my palms over my face. *A dream.*

But even so, I can still remember the joy that filled me when I saw Raine's face. And in that moment I have to forcibly stop myself from running back to Number 36.

Instead, I glance at the many clocks that litter this room. Noon.

So much for my plan to only sleep five minutes. I'd slept through the rest of the night, and half of the day as well. No wonder my head is fuzzy and my dreams strange.

I make myself a cup of coffee, then settle in to work on the inventory. I last about half an hour on that task, but then my mind wanders back to my odd dream.

What the devil did he mean, "Look to yourself?"

I cock my head, suddenly remembering my fifteenth birthday. He'd arranged a full-blown scavenger hunt. Was that what he was doing now?

As soon as the thought enters my head, I cringe. What the hell am I thinking? It was a dream. A stupid dream, not my father actually calling me. Not my dad helping me out.

I should just cash it in and work on the inventory, but now I feel like I'm on a quest, albeit a ridiculous and foolish one.

Look to yourself.

Callie Sinclair.

Could it be that simple?

I head to the bookshelves and look in the C's. Nothing.

I try the S's. Same result.

Apparently, no. It couldn't be that simple.

But then I frown. I've never used my given name; I've always been known by my middle name.

But my first name is Olivia, after my dad.

I go to the O's.

And there, among the tattered covers, is a book with nothing on the spine. Just faded brown leather.

I pull it out, open it.

The first entry is from 2012, and I realize that this is the most current of the series of journals in which my dad wrote his notes about the various pieces he tracked.

The final entry is from last week.

It's curious by its lack of detail, noting only that he had been hired to find a rare amulet. Usually, my father included all known facts about any item he was seeking, including anyone who commissioned the search or who might be an interested buyer.

With this entry, there is nothing other than an additional note scrawled on the bottom like an afterthought:

C—find the rainman. Help him.

With him, what is hidden will be revealed.

I pull the book up to my chest and hug it, and as I do, I realize that I have sunk to the ground. I put the book down beside me and close my eyes.

The rainman.

My father is sending me back to Raine.

And I don't know if I'm relieved or scared.

****

I didn't take a good look at Number 36 last night, and now as I stand in front of it, I take the opportunity to study the red brick building at 36 East 63rd Street. Unlike the wide neighboring buildings with which it shares walls, Number 36 is narrow, with only two windows gracing each of its five stories. The first two floors are convex, as if the building consists of a box sitting atop a cylinder. The brick is a faded red, and the trim around each of the windows is molded plaster, now off-white from so many years of exposure to the elements.

I stand on the street, my hand resting lightly on the iron railing that surrounds the property. Like many brownstones in Manhattan's Upper East Side, the first floor is slightly below street level, and the railing makes a sharp turn and then slopes downward, guiding visitors down five concrete steps to a small courtyard filled with colorful, fragrant blooms.

I have not yet descended those stairs, and yet I have walked past them five times in the last hour, making the trek back and forth between Madison and Park three times, and twice going all the way to Central Park.

Each time I end up back here, as if there is an elastic band around my waist and it is tied fast to this red brick building and the man inside.

Rainer Engel.

It is clear from my father's journal that I need to see him again. And yet, I cannot help the trepidation that grows in me, all the more potent because it is mixed with excitement, anticipation, and most of all, longing.

As much as I have told myself it is best to stay away, to run, I can't escape the simple, basic truth that I want to see him again. I want to touch him and be touched by him.

I don't know what that means, but I do know that I have no more excuses. I can put this off no longer.

Then quit dragging it out. Just go.

I grimace because there is no denying the reasonableness of my own advice. And so I bite the bullet and descend the stairs.

Almost immediately, the din of early afternoon traffic fades and the stale miasma of exhaust and street-side garbage is replaced by the gentle perfume of lavender and jasmine.

It's like entering another world, and I'm honestly not sure if that's good or bad.

The courtyard is lovely, but I barely pay attention to the pots overflowing with flowering vines or the concrete benches set with precision so that there is always at least one seat in the sun and one in the shade. Instead, I move with purpose to the front door. It is solid wood, polished to a shine. A gold knocker in the shape of a bird is mounted at eye level, its trailing tail feathers acting as a handle.

A brass plaque mounted to the brick facade to the right of the door reads:

Dark Pleasures
Est. 1895
Members Only

I don't know what the plaque refers to, but since I do know that Raine lives here, I assume that the residential brownstone was at one time some sort of gentlemen's club, a not uncommon thing back in the nineteenth century, after all.

There is a keypad mounted beneath the plaque, giving the building an anachronistic feel. There doesn't seem to be any sort of bell, however, and so I lift the tail feather and rap sharply on the door.

I hear nothing, but considering how dense the door sounded when I knocked, there could be a brass band playing back there and I wouldn't hear them. A minute passes, then another. I am just raising my hand to knock again when the door opens inward, revealing a white-haired elderly man in black and white livery.

"Madam," he says with a slight bow. "How may I be of service?"

I am not usually the tongue-tied sort, but I'm feeling a bit like I've been tossed backward in time, and it takes a moment for me to thrust myself back into the twenty-first century. I'd assumed this building had been converted to apartments. But considering the limo, now I'm thinking that Raine must own the entire brownstone. "I'm looking for Mr. Engel," I say. "Is he home?"

He studies me for a full minute.

"I didn't realize my question required such thought," I say, then immediately regret it. I'm not generally rude, especially not to staff, but I'm still feeling shaky and this man's odd reaction to a simple question hasn't calmed my nerves.

"May I inquire as to your business?"

I start to snap that it's not *his* business, but manage to bite back my tongue. "I'm Callie Sinclair," I say. "My father is Oliver Sinclair, an antiques dealer. Mr. Engel came to my father's shop yesterday, and I have some information for him regarding a piece he was inquiring about."

"I see. Please, come in." He steps back and holds the door open, allowing me to enter a dark-paneled foyer. The room is shaped like a semicircle, with a set of double-doors facing me from beyond a round marble pedestal. A huge glass bowl sits atop the pedestal, filled with glass pebbles in various shades of red and blue and purple. It's a lovely centerpiece—and provides the only ornamentation in the room—but what makes it truly spectacular is the flame that burns inexplicably inside the bowl, sending tongues of fire licking over the rim, despite the absence of any obvious fuel.

I follow my guide around the pedestal to the doors, and then through them. Immediately, the atmosphere changes. Soft strains of jazz fill the air, along with the muted, almost chocolatey, scent of cigar smoke.

The low buzz of conversation surrounds us, along with the gentle tinkle of ice in crystal. We pass through a lush seating area with low wooden tables surrounded by plump leather chairs. Groups of men and women sit there, sipping drinks and talking earnestly. Many of the men and a few of the women hold the cigars that account for the subtle scent in the air. Considering that the scent is in no way overpowering, I have to assume that there are hidden ventilation systems in the ceiling.

I see a wall of polished wood humidors running perpendicular to a dark mahogany bar behind which is a set of mirrored shelves filled with dozens of bottles of high-end scotch, along with all the standard other distilled liquors as well.

A tall woman in a black sheath dress comes over to greet us. Her gaze skims over me. "Mr. Daley? Is there a problem?"

I realize for the first time how I am dressed. I'd showered before coming here, and now I wear jeans, Converse sneakers, and a T-shirt my father bought me last Christmas that says *Lawyers do it with appeal.*

Bottom line, I really don't fit in.

"I'm sorry," I say. "I didn't realize this was a club or—"

Mr. Daley's sniff cuts me off. "Ms. Sinclair would like to speak to Mr. Engel. Do you know if he is in residence?"

"Callie Sinclair?" she asks, and I nod, a little shocked that this woman I'd assumed to be the club's hostess knows my name. She turns her attention to Mr. Daley. "He's in the VIP room. I'll escort her."

Mr. Daley nods, then leaves.

"I'm Jessica," the woman says, with a bit of a sparkle in her eyes. "It's very nice to meet you."

"Thanks. I'm feeling a little like I fell down the rabbit hole. I thought Raine lived here. I would have dressed better if—"

"You look fine. Come on."

I follow her through the club, with its dark wood and equally dark leather. A few people frown as I pass, obviously noting how out of place I look. Most, however, pay no attention at all. They are drinking and talking with friends, reading the newspaper, chatting on cell phones.

"What is this place? Dark Pleasures?"

"A very select club," Jessica says. "It provides a sanctuary for those who are granted membership. A respite from the world outside. We have resources for the corporate types who want a working lunch, as well as everything necessary to kick back and just relax for a while. Not to mention an excellent jazz band on Friday nights and the most exceptional Sunday brunch in the city."

"And Raine is a member?"

We have paused in front of a solid oak door marked with a gold placard that announces *VIP access only*. Jessica punches a code into the keypad and I hear the lock release. "Raine? Not exactly. You could say he's more like an owner." She pushes the door open. "Please. After you."

I step inside and am immediately struck by the fact that while the basic decor is the same as the area we just left, the similarities end there. This room includes a number of paintings and antiques that I immediately spot as high-end originals. But despite the money that practically oozes from these walls, the area itself seems more low-key than the main part of the club. There is a vibrancy in this room. A sense of camaraderie. As if I have entered someone's living room and not a public club, even a public club that is select in its membership.

The bar in this room is unmanned, so that anyone can simply make a drink, and it is in that direction that Jessica now heads. "Don't just sit there," she says to the stunningly gorgeous man leaning casually against the bar. "Make Ms. Sinclair a drink. Callie," she says, turning to me, "this is Liam."

From what I can see, Liam is one-hundred percent muscle and about the size of an NFL fullback. He has deep-set eyes and a wide mouth. He's clean-shaven, with raven-black hair that he wears long so that it brushes his collar. He's wearing black slacks and a white button-down and looks as wild and dangerous as a fallen angel.

"What's your poison?" Liam asks.

"Scotch. Thanks."

He grins at Jessica as he pours my drink. "She'll fit right in."

I must look confused because Jessica turns to me. "Scotch and cigars. That's what Dark Pleasures is all about. Though I think you'll learn there's so much more to it than that."

"Oh, no, I just need to deliver a message—"

"I'll go get Raine." Liam passes me my drink, then brushes his hand over Jessica's cheek, and I see both heat and affection pass between them. Something hard and cold settles in my gut. Because

I want that, too, and I can't help but fear that I'm going to spend my life making all the wrong choices and never have it.

It suddenly occurs to me that Jessica never told Liam why I was here. "How does he know I'm looking for Raine?"

"It's Liam's job to know everything." She winks. "Makes it damned inconvenient when I'm Christmas shopping." She leads me to two chairs on either side of a small table. "I would introduce you around, but I don't want to scare you off."

"I don't scare easily," I say, though I have to wonder if my words are true. After all, I ran scared from Raine, didn't I?

I turn in the chair to look around. There are four men sitting around a table at the far side of the room. There are papers scattered on the table in front of them, and one—with hair as dark as Liam's, but with a lean, Hollywood bad-boy appearance—is clearly in charge.

"Why so few people?" I ask. "Because it's still too early for the happy hour crowd?"

"The VIP section is extremely exclusive. Consider yourself privileged. We rarely allow guests in at all."

"Oh." I consider that. "And I guess I have a double strike against me since I'm a woman?"

She laughs. "Not in the least. And I'm not the only female VIP member, just the only one who lives permanently on the East Coast. Dagny's in Los Angeles, and Rachel lives in Paris. But on the whole, you're right. A girl gets lonely swimming in a sea of testosterone. Maybe I'll have some company soon."

Her expression is so welcoming and earnest that I can't help but laugh. "You do know I'm just here to talk to Raine about an amulet?"

"And here he is." She nods toward the opposite side of the room from where we entered. I turn in my chair and see that a hinged bookshelf is moving inward to reveal a hidden hallway. And, of course, Raine.

I swallow, suddenly at a loss for words. Yesterday, he'd been dressed casually. Today, I think he could take on corporate

America. As he strides toward me in a perfectly tailored suit, he seems to exude the kind of power and confidence that can make things happen with little more than a glance.

"Hello, Callie," he says, but what I hear is "I want you."

I try to reply, but my mouth is too dry. I remember the drink that Liam poured for me, and I take a sip, grateful for both its burn and its wetness. "I—I found something. About the amulet, I mean."

He tilts his head as if debating a thorny question. Then he sits down across from me, making me realize that somewhere along the way, Jessica slipped off. "All right," he says. "Tell me."

"I found a reference to it in my father's journal. Here." I pull the leather bound book out of my purse and pass it to him.

"The rainman," he says. "Me?"

"I assume so. Does the next part make sense to you? 'With him, what is hidden will be revealed'?"

He shakes his head. "No. It doesn't mean a thing."

I frown. "Are you sure?" I'd been so certain that coming here would solve the riddle, and I'm not doing a good job of hiding my disappointment. Then again, neither is he.

I tilt my head as I watch the emotions play across his face. Confusion. Disappointment. Resolve.

"This is more than just a collector's piece to you, isn't it?" I ask.

"Yes," he says, but then he says no more, and we're left with the silence that hangs between us, thick with possibility.

I slip my hands beneath the table and wipe my palms on my jeans.

"Right. Well, I'm sorry it didn't mean anything to you." I push my chair back and stand. "I should go."

He reaches out and takes hold of my wrist.

"Raine, please." I am aware of nothing except his touch. The rest of the world has simply melted away. "Please," I repeat, a little desperate this time. "I need to go."

"No," he says, then stands. He is right next to me, so close that I can feel his heat, raging like a furnace. And dear god, I want to burn. "There's something I need to tell you."

"I—what?"

"I'm going to kiss you, Callie."

I gasp, surprised and, yes, excited by his words.

"I'm going to kiss you, and then I'm going to touch you. I'm going to explore every inch of you, with my hands, with my lips, with my tongue. And then, Callie, I'm going to fuck you."

I suck in a stuttering breath and curse my own reaction that so pointedly reveals my response to his decadent promises.

"I can do that here or I can take you to my apartment. It's entirely up to you."

"And if I walk away?"

"That's up to you, too. I'm sure you've heard of free will. But make your decision soon. Because I don't intend to wait much longer to strip you bare. And Callie, know one other thing as well. I asked you what you wanted yesterday, and you said me. And yet in the end, you ran. Think hard before you answer me now. Because this time if you choose my bed, I won't let you go without a fight."

My heard is pounding, my body covered with a thin sheen of sweat.

Every ounce of reason within me tells me to run. And yet instinct and desire and something I don't understand tell me to stay.

I do.

And I don't even think it was my decision. He may have spoken of free will, but what good is that against the force of nature that is Rainer Engel?

Chapter 7

Raine watched the decision play across her face, desire warring with rationality, prudence, whatever personal albatross she clung to. He wanted to clutch her hand and tell her to simply go with faith. To believe in *them*.

But those were words he could not say. He wanted her in his bed. Wanted her fully and completely. But he would not press her. Once more, the choice would be hers, and he was forced to wait— feeling pretty goddamn impotent when you got right down to it.

He knew she did not overtly remember being Livia. But he also knew that didn't matter. The essence was within her, and so that meant that on some level she did understand. Did know him. Did remember.

But even if she didn't—even if this woman standing before him had not once been his mate—he would still want her. Callie Sinclair amused and challenged him in ways he didn't understand and hadn't expected.

He was a man who had died a hundred deaths and no longer looked into the dark with fear. But at the moment, he was terrified that she would walk out of this club the same way that she had walked away from the limo.

Even as the thought entered his head, she took a step away from him, as if manifesting all his deepest fears.

"Callie." Her name felt ripped from his throat, and he knew that the anguish in it revealed everything. Frankly, he didn't give a fuck.

She hesitated, then held out her hand for him. "Not here." He saw the mischief in her smile. "I'm not into exhibitionism."

The extent of his relief was such that it almost brought him to his knees.

"Where's your apartment, Raine?"

"Come with me."

He knew that the others were watching the exchange from across the club. Knew that Mal especially was looking on, particularly after what Raine had told him about Livia's essence. It didn't matter, and he didn't care. All he needed right now was to get to the elevator. That was his primary objective, and once satisfied, he could move on to the next.

He held her by the elbow, and even that simple touch overwhelmed him. He hit the release for the hidden door, and the bookcase swung open. He led her through, into the simple but tasteful area that at one time was part of a grand ballroom. Now, it served as a reception area for Phoenix Security, which had its own entrance separate from Dark Pleasures at the rear of the building.

That, however, was not where he was going now, and he led her to the small, cage-style elevator, then pushed the button to call it.

"What floor?" she asked.

"Penthouse," he said. "The club takes up one and two. Three is office space. Four is reserved for out of town members. Five is my private apartment."

Unlike his brethren, who had used the money they'd earned and stockpiled over the years to acquire some of the most exceptional pieces of property across the globe, including the two brownstones adjacent to Number 36, Raine had never felt the need. Before Callie, he hadn't felt much of anything. Now, for the first time, he thought about how sterile his apartment was. And how little time he had spent over the last few millennia thinking about making a home. Why bother when all he wanted to do was check out?

Now, he regretted that. He wished that the place reflected him. He wanted her to know him fully and completely, and in every way possible. And the thought that what she would see first was a set of rooms as empty as his heart had once been ate at his gut.

Not that he could do anything about it now, he thought as the elevator finished its slow descent to the first floor and opened in front of them. The only other option was a hotel, but that was where he took other women. It was not where he would take her.

He pulled open the gate and ushered her in. And the moment he'd set the contraption in motion, he pushed her up against the far wall, his mouth on hers and his hand between her legs. "Tell me you're wet."

"I am."

"Tell me you want me."

"I do."

He backed away, breathing hard but satisfied. But in one quick movement, she caught his hand and tugged him toward her, making his cock twitch with excitement at such palpable evidence of her desire.

"Please, Raine. I want what you promised."

"What I promised? To kiss you?" He trailed his fingers softly over her lips, forcing himself to hold back. "Touch you?" He leaned forward so that his lips brushed the soft skin of her ear. Christ, she smelled good. Like vanilla and honey, and he knew she tasted just as delicious. "To fuck you?"

He both saw and felt her tremble, and by god, if he was a lesser man, he would have come right then.

"The elevator's open." His voice was tight, because damn him, he wanted it too, and the elevator was only now approaching the third floor. "Anyone can see."

"I really couldn't give a fuck."

Her words cut through him, making him harder than he could have imagined. And when he closed his mouth over hers, it was like he'd gone to heaven. The kiss was wild, and her responsiveness drove him even wilder. The fact that she so openly wanted him was sexy as hell, and he fully intended to give her everything she desired. To fuck her until she cried for mercy, and then to hold her close and soft until she begged for more.

Right now, this kiss alone was like sex. Their tongues mating, their bodies crushed together. He knew he must be hurting her, pressed tight against the scroll-style bars of the elevator cage, but he couldn't stop, and she sure as hell wasn't complaining.

When the elevator finally opened in front of his door, they were both gasping for breath. He led her inside and just about lost it when she peeled off her shirt right in the middle of his foyer, then dropped it on the polished stone floor. "Touch me," she said as she followed the shirt with her bra. Her voice was breathy, raw. "And then after that—"

"Bedroom." He pointed in the general direction. "On the bed. Arms and legs spread. I want to be able to see how wet you are when I walk in the room." He watched her eyes as he spoke, saw the way they dilated in response to his command, and felt the tug of pleasure in his groin. He could concede power in the bedroom from time to time, but he would not be doing so tonight. Not when Callie was so clearly turned on by submitting to his wishes.

"And Callie—no touching."

He watched her go, and the tenderness that swept over him was at least as powerful as this relentless sexual desire. She was everything. The pinnacle. The source. The goal.

In truth, he had never felt this strongly before, and his only thought was that his earlier, tamer passion with Livia had been the passion of youth. Or that his memory had faded to spare him lingering pain.

It didn't matter. Right now, all that mattered was Callie. Making her happy. Making her satisfied.

And that was a task to which he would turn his full attention—

and to which he was willing to devote the rest of his life. Which was a very long time indeed.

****

My first thought is that though the apartment we just walked through is sparse and utilitarian, the bedroom suits him, and I can see bits of the man echoed in the furnishings.

The king-size bed is set against a brick wall, across which is a single wooden shelf filled with books. Above that are several black and white photographs of urban skylines. They are stark and beautiful, just like the room itself.

On the left is a wall of windows covered by vertical blinds. On the right is a wall of mirrors, though I can see that Raine's closet is behind the sliding sections.

The floor is a rich, dark wood that is polished to a sheen, and a plush white rug fills the space at the foot of the bed, topped by a bench upholstered in black leather.

With one exception, the room seems perfectly put together, so precise that it could be a hotel or a showroom. But the bed is unmade, and there is something incredibly intimate about the rumpled sheets and tossed back comforter.

I leave the rest of my clothes on the bench, then climb onto the bed, my body trembling with anticipation as I position myself as he directed.

The truth is, I've been trembling since the first moment I met him, mostly from desire, but also a bit from fear.

Right now, there is no fear. There is only the sweet anticipation of knowing that he is coming and that he intends to take the time to very thoroughly fulfill his promise to me—kiss me, touch me, fuck me.

Oh, god.

My thighs are slick with the evidence of my arousal, and though I want to touch myself, I obey his orders and do not.

That restraint only turns me on more, just as his command did.

There is no denying the fact that Rainer Engel is a man who likes to be in control; I saw that the moment he walked into my father's shop.

But what I didn't know then is how much I wanted him to turn that trait to me—and how much I would respond when he did so. How willing I am to surrender to him and let him take me where he wants me to go, trusting that it will be farther than I have ever gone before.

For a woman who usually keeps as tight a control on her sexual encounters as she does her caseload, this is strange territory. But then again, whatever is happening between Raine and me is strange as well. Strange and exciting and wonderful. And dammit, right then, all I want is more.

All I want is Raine.

I start to call out to him, but I manage to hold my tongue. I know damn well why he is taking his time. More than that, it's working. I'm so aroused it's painful, every cell in my body primed.

I am living, breathing anticipation, and I fear that if Raine doesn't walk in here soon, I'll explode simply from wanting him.

"Now that is a pretty picture."

I lift my head to see him leaning negligently against the doorframe, still in that insanely sexy suit.

"Raine."

"I like my name on your lips. I like it better like this, when it's not just a name but a plea. Tell me, Callie, what are you pleading for?"

"You know. It's your promise."

"Remind me."

"Touch me," I say, because he wants me to beg. "Please, please, touch me."

"With pleasure." He moves slowly to the bed, as if we have all the time in the world, but all that does is make me whimper and squirm. "I like you this way. Wanting me. Waiting for me. Wide open for my pleasure and your own. Tell me, Callie. Do you like it, too?"

"Yes." My word is breathy and so soft it seems to float away on the gentle breeze from a slowly turning ceiling fan.

"Why?"

"I—" I pause to think about it, but he shakes his head.

"No. No analysis. No outline. Just tell me."

"Because I never surrender. Because this is safe. Because you want me to, and—"

"Yes?"

"And because it turns me on to please you."

His sensual mouth curves up into an easy smile. "Does it? In that case we have a lot in common. Because it turns me on to please you. To touch you," he adds, "just as I promised. Close your eyes, Callie. Close your eyes and feel."

I do, feeling first the way the bed sags as he gets on beside me. Then I shiver at the first contact of skin against skin as he draws a single fingertip from the base of my throat all the way down, down, down to my sex. He teases me, lightly stroking my clit, then easing his finger deep inside me as my muscles contract violently, wanting even more than he is yet giving me.

My arms are stretched to the side, and I know better than to move them. But I have to fist my hands in the bedclothes in order to stay in place, and as Raine teases and torments me with one simple finger, I dig my heels in, clutch the bedspread, and arch up, seeking both satisfaction and relief, trying to make the sensation of his hand upon me bolder and brighter, and also trying to escape this intense, slow-building torment that is almost like pain in its persistence.

When he withdraws his finger, I sag onto the bed, already exhausted and more turned on than I can ever remember being simply from this sensual touch…and the anticipation of so much more to come.

"I'm going to touch you everywhere, angel. I want your body as aroused as your cunt. So vibrantly aware that I could brush your shoulder and make you come. I want to watch your skin prickle from my touch, your nipples tighten. I want to see the way your belly constricts as you try to hold in pleasure. I'm greedy, angel, and from you I want everything."

As he speaks, he has moved, and now I feel the bed shift again. This time, I hear him set something on the bedside table, and moments later, I feel his palms upon my ribcage. They are oily, and as he moves them over me, stroking and massaging, I lose myself in the pleasure of being tended by this man. A pleasure that only increases when the oil heats from the friction of his hands.

The sensation of the heat and the scent of the oil's spice is somehow both soothing and arousing—but when he teases my nipples, there is nothing soothing at all. Instead, I want to beg him to close his mouth over my breast. To suck my nipples that are now so potently in need of attention. Again, I bite back the urge, and I allow myself to get lost in the near-pain of this pleasure.

I don't know what is in the oil, some type of mint if the scent says anything. But I do know the effect it has on my tender flesh, and as his hands ease up my calf, my thigh, and toward my sex, I can only bite my lip in anticipation, and then cry out his name when he palms my cunt, making my sex heat and tingle, even more needy than before.

But it is when he strokes circles on my clit, making it throb with unfulfilled need, that he almost drives me over the edge. And I whimper as I feel the coming release, but know also that Raine's expert touch will not allow the explosion until he brings it on.

"So slick. So sweet." I hear the struggle for control in his voice and take some satisfaction from that. He may be the one in charge, but I have a hold on him, too. "Christ, angel, I want to drive my cock into you."

"Yes," I whisper. "Please yes."

"I want to possess you," he continues, as if I haven't spoken. "Hard and fast and furious, until there is no question that you are mine. But not yet. Not just yet."

My moan of protest dies in my throat when I feel the brush of his beard stubble against my inner thigh, and then the stroke of his tongue on my sex. He plays with me, his tongue dancing circles over my clit. But then his mouth closes over my sex in a full-on kiss, and his tongue thrusts inside of me. I cry out, surprised by this sensual assault that has only made me more wild, more desperate.

Though my hips buck, he doesn't yield. Just holds me in place, forcing me to accept the sweet torment that he is rendering with his mouth. But as the pleasure grows—as I start to shatter—he pulls back, and I do not have to open my eyes to know that he is grinning wickedly when he says, "Not just yet, angel."

He flips me over, then treats me to another sensual massage, though this time he focuses mostly on my shoulders and back. Eventually he moves to my thighs, but there are no more small caresses that come close to my sex. No touch that is going to send me over the edge.

And somehow, because I am waiting for it, the absence of such erotic caresses arouses me even more.

"On your knees, angel," he says, and I scramble up, eager for whatever he has in mind next. My mind is awhirl, my body at his disposal. And when he eases me down to the foot of the bed and pulls me toward him so that my rear brushes his slacks, I realize what he intends, and my sex clenches with greed.

I hear the distinct metallic sound of his zipper, then feel the pressure of one hand upon my rear as his other teases my sex.

He starts slowly, opening me. Entering me. He keeps his hands on my waist so that he can control the way I move. But the pleasure is too much for both of us, and his tempo increases with the heightening pleasure.

He bends over me, so that I feel him inside me and on my back. Now he has one hand on my breast and the other teasing my clit as he thrusts hard and deep, and I rock backward to meet him, wanting him to go deeper, wanting him to fill me up completely.

He is fully clothed, and there is something so decadent about me being naked and him being dressed that it adds to my arousal. "You're mine," he says as I fly. "Mine," he repeats as I go spinning off. And when he finally explodes inside me, he takes me with him, and it is as if he has catapulted the two of us to the stars.

And then, when he pulls out and lays beside me, drawing me in to curl against him, I say the one thing that I know he wants to hear: *"Yours."*

Chapter 8

He leads me into the shower, then cleans me up, washing my hair and tending to me so that I feel wonderfully cherished. Afterwards, he dries me off with a fluffy towel then wraps me in a robe that smells like him. I breathe deep, relishing the scent of it. We end up on the couch, wrapped up lazily in each other's arms as we flip through the television channels in a ritual that I would consider uncomfortably domestic with any other man, but with Raine feels just right.

He stops on a football game, and I have to laugh. "Seriously?"

He lifts his brows in mock offense. "You'd prefer what?"

"We passed at least a dozen great movies. *Singin' in the Rain*? How can you resist Donald O'Connor?"

"Actually, I never could. The man's as charming in person as he is on screen."

I cock my head, amused. "Is he?"

For a moment, he looks surprised, then his expression clears and he brushes his finger teasingly down my nose. "I read a lot of biographies. O'Connor's one of my favorite stars." As if to prove the point, we back up to the movie, and he holds me close, then kisses me softly when the movie ends with the billboard of Gene Kelly and Debbie Reynolds.

I sigh. "A shame the world doesn't break out in song like that." I see him watching me and narrow my eyes. "What?"

"I adore the way you think. And I also promise that you don't want me breaking into song. I would scare small animals."

I laugh, but I also can't help the little tingle of pleasure at the compliment.

He clicks off the television then stands, holding out his hand for me.

"Are we dancing?"

He pulls me into his arms and dips me. "That wasn't my original plan, but I can certainly see it as a possibility." He starts to hum, then spins me before moving me artfully around the room. Considering I can't dance to save my life, I'm impressed by his ability to lead, and by the time he dips me again by the bedroom door and then draws me back up for a kiss, I'm laughing and clinging to him, feeling happier and freer than I have since I came home to New York after my dad's stroke.

"Thanks," I say.

"For what?"

I want to say for making this about more than sex, but that seems both odd and presumptuous. "For making life a movie musical, even if just for a few minutes."

He studies my face, and in that moment I am certain that he knows what I had originally intended to say. But all he does is brush a kiss over my lips. "Get dressed," he says. "And let me get you some food."

I half-expect that he's going to cook, but he laughs off that prospect, assuring me that cooking is not in his repertoire. As it's not in mine either—and since the mention of food has reminded me that I am starving—I defer to his suggestion that we go back to the club.

"It's not formal, but jeans and T-shirts aren't allowed. Not even in the VIP area. We decided a long time ago that we needed to keep a certain feel within the place."

"Sadly, I didn't pack a bag."

"You're about Jessica's size," he says, heading out of the bedroom and down the hall to a guest suite. "She won't mind if you borrow something."

I hesitate, not wanting to seem possessive of him so soon, but feeling entirely possessive anyway. And wildly jealous. I *liked* Jessica, after all. And what the hell was she doing leaving her clothes all over Raine's apartment, especially when she was so obviously attached to Liam? And why—

"You're thinking so loudly I can hear every word."

I scowl up at him, still determined not to say a word because it would make me seem petty and jealous. Even though it is obvious that he is reading my face just fine, and I already seem petty and jealous.

"She and Liam moved to a loft in the Village two years ago. They thought it would be an adventure. But when I'm out of town, they sometimes stay here. It seemed easier for them both to just leave some things in the guest room."

"Oh." I clear my throat, feeling foolish. "That makes sense."

A grin dances on his lips.

"What?"

"I like it that you're jealous." His voice is low, with enough heat that it is clear he likes it very much.

"Oh," I say again, but this time it's not foolishness I'm feeling, but something much more provocative. I rise up on my toes and kiss him. "You can fuck me again," I say boldly. "But first you have to feed me."

He laughs. "Then get dressed and let's get some food."

I pick out a knee-length blue dress with a full skirt and matching blue flats. I'm still uncomfortable about borrowing Jessica's clothes, but Raine must have given her a heads-up because the first thing she does when I walk in is make me do a circle, and then sigh.

"Well, damn. I think you look better in it than I do."

Since Jessica is one of the most beautiful women I've ever seen, I doubt that. But I'm no slouch either, and I'm willing to concede that I look hot.

There's a phone by the bar that calls the kitchen, and Raine orders us both burgers and fries, and I have to smile at the dichotomy between the atmosphere and the food. But I like it. It makes the club comfortable rather than stuffy, and it bolsters my initial impression that this is the place where friends gather.

As I sit in one of the plush leather armchairs and look around, I have to say that I think that is true. As far as I can tell, the men are all close, and Jessica moves seamlessly among them. Friends with each. And much more than friends with Liam. There's only one, in fact, who shoots both Raine and me a flat look before leaving the room not long after we enter.

"Who was that?" I ask when Jessica comes over. "I got the impression he and Raine aren't going to be doing the guy bonding thing anytime soon."

"Trace. And you're right."

"What happened?"

Jessica waves the question away. "Ancient history, so don't worry about it. And Trace is only in New York a few more days. He divides his time between here, Los Angeles, and Paris."

"Nice."

"He doesn't like feeling tied down. At any rate, I'm being paged." She waves to Liam, who is tapping his wristwatch. "And Raine is coming back with your burgers." Her smile is just a little bit wicked. "Have fun, you two."

The burgers are as delicious as burgers in an exclusive, centuries-old club should be, and the company is just as awesome. Mal and Dante join us, and we talk about everything from old movies to architecture and even a few quick references to the company they all work for, Phoenix Security, though the comments are vague enough that I have no sense of what the company actually does.

As we talk, Mal and Raine play a game of chess, and though I keep my expression neutral, I'm secretly thrilled when Raine wins.

"Anyone for another drink?" Dante asks as he rises.

"No thanks," I say, then notice the time on the ornate clock on the far wall. "Actually, I should go. I want to see my dad tonight. And I should probably work on the inventory a bit, too."

"All right," Raine says.

"All right?"

"I'll come with you. Hospital. Inventory. I can't think of a better way to spend an evening."

"Broadway comes to mind," I tease. "But I'm glad you're such an easy date."

"So long as I'm with you, you'll find I'm very easy."

I see Mal and Dante exchange looks and have to laugh. "Your friends are going to think I have you wrapped around my little finger."

"That's okay," Raine says, standing and offering me a hand. "You do."

The hospital is a short walk from Number 36, but Dad is sleeping when we get there.

"When he's awake, I read to him or just talk," I tell Raine. "But I don't want to wake him."

"We'll come back tomorrow."

I glance at him, grateful this is an outing he's willing to repeat. "Thanks. I'd like that."

Once we're back on the sidewalk, I glance sideways at him. "So you're home during the afternoon and tomorrow you have time to go with me to the hospital. You drive around in a limo and live in the penthouse apartment of one of the nicest brownstones I have had the pleasure of visiting. Forgive me, Mr. Engel, but what kind of a company is Phoenix Security? Or are you simply one of the glorious elite who lives off piles of money gathered by the family over the last gazillion centuries?"

"As a matter of fact, I do have those piles of money gathered over centuries. They provide a nice cushion and allow me to buy roses from street vendors without breaking my budget." He stops at a street vendor and does exactly that.

"Thank you, kind sir," I say, taking the rose he hands me.

"But Phoenix also provides a nice income."

"So what does the company do? By security, you don't mean stocks and bonds, right? You're talking about stuff like wiring people's houses? Motion detectors and video surveillance?"

He looks amused. "Not stocks, correct. But as for the other, I'd say that we're more...specialized. The company's been around a very long time. We provide exclusive services on an international scale."

"Sounds exotic."

"It can be."

"Dangerous?"

"That too."

"Well, what do you know?"

His brow furrows. "What?"

"Turns out I'm falling for James Bond."

"Is that right?" He's laced his voice with a British accent and I laugh, delighted.

"Do you mean *is that right* that you're really like James Bond?" I ask. "I couldn't say. You haven't given me enough details of your missions."

He lifts our twined hands to his lips and kisses my fingers. "I mean, is it right that you're falling for me."

"Oh." I bite my lower lip, then tilt my head up to smile at him. "Yeah. That's right."

"That's very interesting information."

"I'm very glad you think so." I can't seem to banish the grin that is determined to spread across my face.

"I think it's fair to say the feeling is mutual."

I ease up next to him as he hooks his arm around my shoulders. "I like this," I say. "It's been ages since I've just walked around the city, and even when I was living here, I never seemed to come to the park enough."

"Nor do I."

"I have a radical idea," I say. "Let's blow off inventory and just continue what we're doing."

"I love your radical idea."

"I'm glad. I forget how nice it is to just look around sometimes."

He nods. "Funny that I have all the time in the world and yet I never seem to find the time to enjoy it."

His words hit me like a sting, and I tug him to a stop. "What do you mean, all the time in the world?" I know he can't be speaking literally. And yet for some reason I don't understand, his words have shaken me.

His brow furrows, and I think that he must be as confused by my reaction as I am. "I just mean that I've filled my days with work when I should be filling them with this. The park. A stroll. A beautiful woman by my side."

He presses a kiss to my temple and I squeeze his hand in response, feeling just a little bit foolish about the direction my thoughts were going.

"And you? Do young, brilliant assistant district attorneys manage to fit love and leisure into their lives?"

"Very little leisure, even less love." I tilt my head so that I am looking at him, knowing that my next words are probably inexcusably bold. "Before now, love was never on my radar."

His smile is slow and easy and full of both heat and understanding. "Is that so?"

"It is." And because now I'm starting to feel a little too exposed, I take his hand and urge him further into the park, aiming us along the trails toward Central Park South.

"Thanks again for coming with me to see my dad." It's my best effort to change the subject. "What about your parents? Where do they live?"

"They're gone." I hear the loss clearly in his voice. "It's been a very long time."

"I'm so sorry." We have arrived at the end of the park, and now we step out onto the sidewalk. I glance around, then smile. "Your parents, my dad. I think we could both use some cheering up. Come on."

I lead him to Fifth Avenue and FAO Schwarz, then wave my finger in an *ah-ah* gesture when he starts to protest. "Haven't you seen *Big?* The big piano is an instant mood enhancer."

"Better than sex?" he deadpans.

"No, but we can do it in public without getting arrested." I tug his hand. "Come on."

As it turns out, we have to wait in line for ten minutes behind a gaggle of seven- and eight-year-olds. We are, by about two decades, the oldest people in line.

Frankly, I don't care. And after I start out doing a truly crappy job of playing *Mary Had a Little Lamb* by hopping from one note to the next, Raine joins me and, as expected, completely shows me up by playing the opening riff of *The Entertainer.* And getting a standing ovation from everyone in the store.

Honestly, it's pretty cool.

And as we step back outside and start up Fifth Avenue toward 63rd Street and Number 36, I can't help but think that this is the most fun I've ever had with a man. For that matter, it's the most fun I've had with anyone in a very, very long time, and I'm quite sure that my grin makes that very, very clear.

"Home?" Raine asks, and I nod automatically.

It's only when we have reached Number 36 and are back in the penthouse that I realize that this is where I expected we were going. And yet this isn't home. Not for me.

But still...

"What is it?" Raine asks, seeing me pause by the window.

"Nothing," I say. "It's just—you came here, and that felt right to me. And I—"

"You feel it, too." He moves closer to me, and that heat that always seems to be bubbling beneath the surface with us seems to crackle and pop. "That tug. That connection."

I nod slowly. I know exactly what he means. "It should scare me. But it doesn't."

"Maybe it would with someone else. Maybe it doesn't scare you because it's right with me."

"I think it is," I say. "Right, I mean." I press my hand to the glass. "This is moving so fast, Raine, but it doesn't feel strange. It feels as though I've known you forever. As if—I don't know. As if we're picking up where we left off somehow."

He is staring at me, his expression managing to be both earnest and astounded.

I shake my head and hold up my hand. "I'm sorry. That was way too much. I shouldn't have said anything. I don't want you to feel weird or think that I'm moving too fast." I'm rambling, but I don't care. "I just wanted to tell you that, and now I'm thinking that maybe I should have just stayed quiet, because I really don't know where that came from."

"Livia," he says.

"What?" I have no idea what that means.

"Where it came from. It came from Livia."

I lick my lips, an odd sensation twisting inside me, almost like fear. As if I do understand—but I just don't want to.

"What are you talking about?"

He shakes his head. "No, I'm sorry. I shouldn't have said anything."

"Why not? If you understand what's happening between us, why we're moving so fast, why it feels so right, then please tell me. I want to know."

I can see the debate play out on his face, but I don't understand it. Or, at least, I don't understand it until he finally speaks.

"She was my mate," he says, and I stand completely frozen. "My wife. Many years ago. She died, Callie. But part of her lives inside you."

I force myself to breathe in and out. Is this a joke? Because I pushed him to tell me something before he was ready?

"You're saying your dead wife was what? Reincarnated inside me? That the reason you're attracted to me is because I'm walking around with your dead wife hitching a ride?"

"Reach inside, Callie." His voice doesn't waver in the least, and I realize that this isn't a joke. He believes this bullshit. And I'm not sure if I should sit down and cry or run away in terror. "Search for the core of our connection, and you'll know I'm telling you the truth. It's why this feels so right."

I shake my head, not quite sure I can manage words right now.

"Please," he presses. "Don't you see? It explains why it feels to you as if we're picking up where we left off."

"*No.*" The word is ripped out of me. "All this explains is why I was so scared of finding a man I connected with in the first place. Because all that does is open me up to nut jobs. *Fuck.*" I slam my palm against the window so hard I'm surprised the glass doesn't break.

"*Shit.*" He runs his fingers over his scalp. "Dammit, Callie, I'm sorry. I shouldn't have said anything yet. But I thought…I know you feel it as profoundly as I do. I thought you would understand it, too. And it's so damn easy to talk to you that I forget that your perspective is so much different than mine."

"Perspective?" I repeat. "You mean the view from sanity?" I am blinking madly, trying to hold back tears. I'm destroyed. That's the bottom line. Everything I wanted. Everything I let myself believe, and it's all gone in one puff. Like pulling back the wizard's curtain to reveal the truth.

I force myself to draw a deep breath and keep my voice from shaking. "I'm sorry, Raine. Whatever you feel, it isn't real, and I'm not going to ride along just to be part of your game. Because I can tell you right now, there's no way that I can win."

Chapter 9

My head is swimming as I stumble out of the service entrance off of Raine's kitchen. I find myself in a whitewashed corridor, and I turn frantically, looking for an elevator. It is at the end of the hall on my left, and I race that direction, then jab the button. I press my forehead to the wall next to the elevator and will myself not to cry. And I pray that Raine doesn't come after me, because right now, I don't know what I would do.

His mate? He'd thought he'd lost me? Her? I carry her essence inside me?

It was insane.

In a rush, I remember my fear that first night in the limo. That my desire for him was only an illusion.

It turns out that wasn't what I should have feared—*my* desire is real.

It is Raine's desire for me that is an illusion.

And this is all some sort of horrible psychological mind-fuck wherein he thinks I'm his dead wife or something.

It breaks my heart. And, yeah, it scares me, too. Because I'd thought what he felt was real.

And because he so obviously believes that what he said is true.

Oh god, oh god, oh god, how could I have been so stupid? How could I have let myself get so close because now it feels like he's taken a knife and sliced me in two?

The elevator doors open and I hurry inside, then jab the button to make the doors close.

But it is not even the knowledge that I allowed this to happen that eats at me the most. That I broke my own rules and allowed myself to get burned.

No, the worst is something I can barely admit, even to myself. And that is the tiny, buried, lingering feeling that he's telling the truth. That he believes it not because he went over the deep end in grief, but because it is true.

Damn me, he's gotten so under my skin—he's managed to twist me up so completely and thoroughly—that I am actually tempted to buy into his psychosis. I can almost even convince myself that I feel it, too, some deep primal connection that extends back to even before he walked into my father's shop.

But that's absurd. And despite my childhood searches for fairies and angels, I know better than to think that such things truly happen.

Don't I?

I'm still lost in my confused and swirling thoughts when I hit the street. It's dark, but not terribly late. Still, the street seems strangely empty, as if everything has shifted and I'm now living in some sort of netherworld that traps people whose dreams have died.

I don't like it, and all I want is to get to the shop, go upstairs, and sleep for a year.

I hurry that way, intent on my goal.

So intent, in fact, that I let my guard down. Which is why I have only myself to blame when the burly man in a windbreaker jumps out from the small passage between the shop and the next building.

I barely have time to make a sound before he has a hand over my mouth and has yanked me into the shadow-filled corridor. A cold sweat breaks out over my skin and my heart is pounding so hard I can hear nothing other than my own blood thrumming through my veins. In fact, I only realize that he is talking to me when he shakes me and I see his mouth moving.

"The amulet, bitch. Where the fuck is the amulet?"

"I—I have no idea." I have always had the illusion that I would be strong in a fight. But I'm not strong now. I'm terrified and it is all that I can do to focus and breathe so that the world doesn't turn to gray and I pass out right now.

I pray that someone passing by will see or hear us. The passage is filled with trash bins, and because of that, we are only a few feet off the lit sidewalk. But the night is quiet, and as far as I know, we are all alone.

"You don't know? You don't *know*? Well, maybe this will remind you." He pulls a knife from his pocket and thrusts the blade toward me. But he doesn't even make it an inch before something that looks like a thin strip of flat red light lashes out in front of me, slicing not only through his chest, but right through the metal blade as well.

The scream that I'd been holding in erupts, and I whip around to find Raine holding something that would be a sword if the blade didn't appear to be made out of…what? Light? Flame? Heat?

I don't know. Frankly, I don't care. I'm just grateful that he's there, and I take an unsteady step toward him. As I do, I hear the sharp report of a gunshot, then see the shock on Raine's gorgeous face.

He steps forward as if drunk, then turns. As he does, I see a second man, standing less than a foot away.

"Stay…the fuck away…from her." Raine's words sound like they are being forced out through water, and I run toward him even as he manages a burst of strength and spins, thrusting that strange sword right into the gunman's heart before yanking the blade free and collapsing onto the ground, blood gushing out of the bullet wound that has opened his back.

The gunman falls, too, but I am not concerned about him. I only care about Raine.

But though I try to get to him, it is as if I have hit a wall of air, and I can't move forward. *Shock*, I think. *I'm in shock.*

And then, when his body begins to rise and spin and burn, I am certain that it is shock and that I am hallucinating.

And the last thing I remember before the world goes gray is Raine's body, black and charred as it writhes in dancing tongues of fire.

* * * *

"So you just told her?" It's Mal's voice, but it seems as if it's floating in a cloud above me. "What? You had her in bed and that was your idea of pillow talk? You tell her she's got the essence of your dead mate inside her? No wonder she bolted."

"Boys…" Jessica's voice now, stern yet hushed.

"An error in judgment, I admit," Raine says, his voice soft. *He's alive. Dear god, he's alive.* "She said she felt the connection, that it seemed to her as if we were picking up where we left off. And I just couldn't—"

"What?" Liam asks. "Couldn't wait to terrify the girl?"

I try to open my eyes, to see Raine. To touch him. To tell them all that I'm in here, but I can't seem to get any part of me to function properly. I'm trapped inside myself, and I want so desperately to come back.

"Stop it, you two. When was the last time you saw Raine so happy? And she's the reason for it. Of course he wants her to understand. And you," she continues. "Do you love me?"

"You know I do," Liam says.

"So you'll share your crazy-shit beliefs and ideas with me and expect me not to bolt, right?"

Liam says nothing.

"That's what I thought. Of course you will. So cut him some slack. Both of you. The man's in love, and love makes men fools.

And as for you," Jessica continues, and from her softening tone, I am sure she has turned her attention back to Raine. "She may have felt it, but she doesn't really get it. You, Rainer Engel, have been alive for thousands of years, but you've forgotten how to be subtle. So go easy on her, okay? And just keep reminding yourself that she doesn't understand any of this yet."

She's right, I think. I don't understand. But I want to. Because unless everyone at Number 36 is as crazy as I thought Raine was, then it's me who is missing the bigger pictures, and not them.

I saw Raine burn and yet he is alive. And now Jessica is saying he's been alive for thousands of years.

So yeah, it's fair to say I don't get it. But I very much want to.

"Thanks, Jessica," Raine says.

"You're welcome. And now, gentlemen, I think we should leave."

"It's okay. You don't have to."

"Yes," she says. "We do. Look." Her voice softens and I feel a gentle pressure as she takes my hand and squeezes my fingers. "Welcome back, Callie. You're going to be just fine."

"Callie?" Raine's voice is urgent, and it is his hand I feel next. Strong and warm and safe. Despite everything—or maybe because of everything—I am certain that he will keep me safe.

"Come on, angel. Open your eyes. I'm fine, and you're fine, and I need you to open your eyes. Everything else can wait, but I need to see you. I need to know that you're okay."

I hear the urgency in his voice, the fear and the pain, and it twists at my heart. And somehow I manage to claw my way up through the fog.

My eyes flutter open, and the first thing I see is Raine's gorgeous face. The tight line of his mouth matching the worry in his eyes. And then it fades, and those beautiful blue irises shine even as his mouth curves into a smile of pure relief.

"Thank god," he says, then lifts my hand to his mouth and gently kisses my palm.

"You came after me."

"I did. I almost didn't. I've told myself so many times that no matter how much I want and need you, that I can't force your hand. And yet I couldn't simply stay back. Not with you running from me in fear. I had to at least make sure you were okay."

"I wasn't. Those men." I shudder. "Thank you."

"It was my pleasure. Except of course for the dying part. That is never much fun."

"That really happened?" My voice is coarse, my throat raw. "I didn't hallucinate? You really burned?"

"I really burned."

I frown, trying to wrap my mind around that, then take a sip from the glass of water he holds for me. As he bends close, I see the wing of a bird peeking out from his collar to rise up his neck. "That's new," I say, reaching out to stroke it.

"It is. *La petite mort*, as you said. With each death, I get a new mark."

I shake my head. "I feel like this should be making sense, but it's not. The only thing I'm sure of is that you were telling me the truth—although I still don't entirely understand what that truth is. And I didn't believe you. I'm sorry."

"You have no reason to be," he says as I scoot up on the bed, moving back to make room for him beside me. I take the opportunity to look around and don't recognize the room.

"The guest quarters. I wasn't sure you'd want to go back to my room."

I can't help but smile. Even with the horrible things I said to him, he is still taking care of me.

I draw a breath. "So back up. You die. And when you do you burn? And when you burn you get a tattoo?"

"A nice summary, though it leaves out some of the finer points." He traces up and down my fingers, and though I don't pull my hand away, the contact is both intimate and distracting. "What do you know of alternative dimensions?"

"About as much as you know about Tom Hanks' movies."

I'm grateful for the smile that flickers on his lips. "Then I'll give you the concise version. There are other dimensions that exist parallel to ours, and with the right technology, they can be traveled. In my world, a very long time ago, I was part of an elite team sent to recover a malevolent energy that had become uncontained."

"A bad guy."

"Very much."

"In our dimension, energy is sentient." He frowns, obviously trying to figure out how to make that more clear. "You don't need a body. You just need what in your world might be called a soul."

"No body? No physical love."

"Not as you understand it. No skin on skin, body against body. But that didn't mean we couldn't feel passion, connection, sensuality. Even climax. It just means that there is no point of reference that can help me explain what it is like to make love in my dimension."

"I feel like I should understand," I admit. "Like I almost do, even. As if I'm reaching for something in a dream."

"Livia," he says, and I nod. Because like it or not, I now believe that is true, though I am no closer to fully understanding it.

"So you didn't have a body?"

"Again, it's difficult to explain. Yes, and no. We had form inside the consciousness. Like an avatar. Or a dream. It wasn't until we arrived here in this dimension and on this planet that we acquired this human form." He grins. "And while I will not say that one is better than the other, I will say that the pleasure that can be had with a body of flesh and blood rises to a level that I never imagined in my youth."

I smirk. "You must have liked it. From my perspective, I'm willing to bet you had a lot of practice."

He smiles in response, and I know that I'd said the right thing, lightening the moment just a bit. Because this is heavy stuff we are talking about, and though I know I won't understand all of it, I am trying. Both to understand, and to believe.

"So you became human after you chased the energy—"

"We call it the fuerie."

I nod. "Okay. So you chased it to this dimension?" I'm proud of myself for keeping that much straight, and I say a silent thank you to reruns of *Star Trek* and my love of science fiction movies.

"Exactly. You don't need to know all the details, and to be honest, I don't want to relive them. Suffice it to say that there was an accident. We crashed here, on earth, and so did the fuerie. We melded with a party of traveling warriors and wise men and women sent by an Egyptian prince to follow a comet they had seen racing across the sky."

"You."

"Us," he affirms. "I'm human now, albeit immortal."

I nod, figuring that I could get more details on all of that later. "And the bad guy?"

"It crashed nearby and forced itself—or bits of itself— into unwilling human shells before riding to our location to attack." He drew in a breath. "The battle was hard-fought and many of the humans who had traveled with the warriors' party were killed, and many of the fuerie escaped. And until we can reopen the void and send it back, it is our duty to track down the fuerie and destroy it, in whatever form or forms it has taken."

"You can send it back?"

"The amulet your father was searching for is the last of seven pieces that can reopen the void and direct the fuerie back to our dimension."

"So that's why you wanted it."

"That," he says. "And so that I could go back."

"Go back?" Something cold, like dread, washes over me. "You're going away?"

"No." The word is harsh and firm and I am instantly relieved. "Not anymore. But I won't lie to you. I've been lost. Reckless. I wanted to get back because I thought Livia was lost during the battle. The fuerie created a rift, and I thought that she'd been thrust into it. I thought she was gone. Neither in this dimension nor any other." He meets my eyes. "For creatures made of pure energy, that is the essence of death."

I nod. "So you were grieving."

"I was, yes. But it was more than that." He runs a hand over his head. "In our world, when two beings mate, it is a permanent melding that even death doesn't shatter. How could it when, for beings of pure energy, death does not exist?"

I frown, not sure I'm following.

"Don't you see? I was grieving for Livia, true. But I was also grieving for myself, and my knowledge that I would spend eternity alone."

I suck in a breath as understanding washes over me. "That's heartbreaking."

"It's part of who we are. Or who we were. Those of us in the brotherhood aren't truly one or the other anymore." An ironic smile tugs at his mouth. "It's a brave new world."

Since I don't know what else to do, I squeeze his hand, and am gratified when he squeezes back.

"And in all this time, you never once felt her presence?"

"Not once. But keep in mind that the world is a very big place. And three thousand years passes in the blink of an eye to a creature made purely of energy. Even to those of us in the brotherhood, time moves at a different pace than for pure humans."

"I think my head is spinning. I want to understand it all, but I have so many questions and all the answers are coming at me at once."

"I know. Suffice it to say that for a very long time, I was lost. I was reckless. When I lost hope that we would ever find the final amulet, I chased death. I took unnecessary risks."

"But you're just reborn," I point out. "Not fun, maybe. But why is it a risk?"

"I wanted the pain," he says, his voice so low I can barely hear it. "And eventually, I wanted to just be hollow."

I shake my head. "I don't understand."

"A body can only take so many deaths. Then something switches, usually with no warning. I had a warning tonight. I am running out of free passes. Too many more burns and I will be hollow, my humanity lost."

I swallow as cold fingers of fear grab me. "You risked that for me?"

"I would risk more than that for you."

"Because of Livia," I say flatly.

"Some part of her essence is inside you, yes. We call it transference."

"And that's different than you? The way you—what did you call it?—melded with the wise men?"

"The prince was a man who had visions, and he had sent his wise men prepared and with a mission. We merged with them at a genetic, bodily level, and with their consent. But transference remains a process of energy. Like you think of a soul. Or what you might call reincarnation."

The thought makes me shiver. "So she's just there? Inside me?"

"Yes and no." He frowns. "These things aren't easy to understand or explain. She is there, yes, because energy can neither be created nor destroyed."

"Einstein."

"He got that right, yes. But it can be changed. And at least some of Livia—of her essence—is part of you. Inseparable now. And dormant, though that is the wrong word, as it suggests she is only sleeping and could wake and take over. She can't. She is you and you are her."

I hug myself, feeling overwhelmed. What I'm not, however, is freaked out.

I'm not entirely sure if that's a good sign or a bad.

"You thought she was gone." I pause because I'm trying to organize my thoughts. "But she didn't know you believed that. She thought you left her."

"I suppose."

"No," I say with certainty. "She did." I meet his eyes. "I think that fundamental belief is an ingrained part of me. Not just because my mother left me, but because that fear of being loved and then pushed away is deep inside me."

"Oh, god, Callie." The pain is clear in his voice.

"It's not your fault," I say. "It was a mistake. And honestly, I'm glad to understand."

Raine, however, looks unconvinced, and very guilty.

Since that wasn't my intent, I cast about for another question. "The men who attacked me—why were they looking for the amulet?"

"The fuerie was inside them. They want to open the void as well. If they have all the pieces of the amulet, they can escape this world and run wild across all dimensions. If we have all the pieces, we can send them back through to a containment center. Or we could open a rift and thrust them into the netherworld between dimensions, essentially destroying them."

I nod, thinking that over. "Okay. But how do you know for sure the fuerie was in them? Maybe it was just an old-fashioned mugging."

"I could see it in them."

That surprises me. "Really? So does that mean you can see Livia, too?"

"No. As I said, you and she are one, though I can feel her essence in the core of you. In order to survive, Livia made a choice all those years ago. The fabric of your dimension doesn't allow us to remain unbound as energy for long. So Livia had to either allow her energy to merge with a human's, or fill the human and remain separate. But that is violent and disrespectful, and is not our way. It is what the fuerie did."

"Possession," I say. "When you hear a story about demonic possession, it is the fuerie?"

"More often than not," he affirms. "As much as I've told you, I'm still only scratching the surface."

I nod because I've already figured that out. How could he possibly explain in just one conversation everything there is to know about how beings of pure energy interact with our world?

I cast about for a less complicated question. "So when you see the fuerie, what does it look like?"

"Flame. Heat. Energy. It's the foundation of our world. You could have seen it too, if you were properly trained. I'm surprised you didn't, actually, since you were scared. Often adrenaline triggers the reflex."

I frown because something about that sounds familiar. I can't imagine why, though, and I temporarily push the thought away. Right now, I'm about to go into information overload. Still, I can't stop asking questions. "You killed them? With that weird blade?"

"A fire sword. It's a weapon of the Phoenix Brotherhood. I go nowhere without it."

"You don't really have a security company."

Now his grin turns boyish. "Absolutely we do. And we have one hell of an elite clientele. It's a useful cover for our search for the fuerie. And many of our cases are entirely legit and unconnected to our original mission."

"So can I see it? The fire sword."

He laughed. "It burned in the fire. Usually I manage to toss it clear before collapsing, but not this time. I'll have to forge a new one. But I promise to let you watch."

We share a smile, and I feel something between us click back into place. I like it. And something in that gentle moment triggers the thought I'd been searching for earlier.

"Dad told the paramedic he saw a face in flames."

I can tell I've hit on something interesting by the expression on Raine's face. "Did he?"

"Why could he see them if you have to have some of your world's energy inside you?"

"Because of you."

"Me?"

"Livia."

"Oh." Automatically, I hug myself, then tug the blanket up higher on my legs.

"I think she must be attached to your family."

I nod because things are starting to make sense. "So when Daddy came to me in a dream, it was real?"

"It was real," Raine says. "And you can speak to him as well." He squeezes my hand. "It will be dreamlike at first, but with time you can communicate as easily as talking."

It takes me a second to process what he's saying. "So even if Daddy doesn't wake up—"

"So long as he's in there, he can get out."

I close my eyes, and warm tears spill down my cheeks. "He knows that, I think." I sniff and wipe the tears, then manage a watery smile. "He gave me a clue about where to find the journal. It was filed under my name. Not C, but O." I meet Raine's eyes, then hesitate, not sure I want to tell him the rest.

His brow creases with a frown. "What?"

I take a breath and tell him. "My given name is Olivia."

For a moment, he just looks at me. "And your father is Oliver." He nods as a slow smile spreads across his face. "Another piece of the puzzle slips into place."

He shakes his head as if in amazement. "Dear god, I have loved you for an eternity, and I will never lose you again."

He pulls me close and holds me tight, but despite the fire that I now know burns in this man, I still feel cold, and the shiver that runs through me is one of apprehension and fear. And, I think, of loneliness.

Chapter 10

An hour later, I'm curled up in one of the plush leather recliners in the VIP room at Dark Pleasures. Beside me, Jessica is telling me about the last mission she went on with Liam.

"To Prague, which was an absolute treat as we stayed a week even after the job was done. We'd lived there once, but that was well before indoor plumbing, and this was a big improvement."

I like the stories, and I definitely like Jessica, but I feel as though she thinks she knows me, but of course she doesn't. Livia, perhaps. But I am not her. And I can't help but fear that all of the brethren, Jessica included, have forgotten that very basic fact.

Across the room, Liam and Dante are bent over the chessboard while Raine and Mal are deep in conversation at a small table tucked into a corner.

After a few moments, Raine comes over, and I hold out my hand. He bends to kiss me in greeting, the gesture warm and comfortable and familiar.

"They all think they know me." The words are out before I have time to think about them, and I realize that this has been bothering me more than I have let myself realize.

"You're mine. Of course they want to know you."

"They think they already do."

He nods slowly. "But that's true. At the core of it, at least." He bends to kiss me, and I curl my arms around his neck, wanting something more from him, though I'm not sure what.

"I love you," he whispers, voicing the words for the very first time. But instead of filling me, the words seem to hang heavy inside me.

"I love you, too," I say, then brush a kiss over his lips to camouflage my confusion and strange, dark thoughts. I shift in my chair, then lever myself up, feeling suddenly antsy. I smile, as if there is nothing in the world on my mind, and ask him if he wants a drink. Then while he takes the chair, I go to the bar and pour myself a shot. I toss it back, and as I do, I see my reflection in the mirror behind the bar.

Me.

Callie Sinclair.

So why do they all see Livia?

I look harder, and I cannot deny that I can find her inside me. The truth is there—Livia is part of me. Her core. Her essence. Her soul. Whatever you want to call it, it has become a part of me. And perhaps that piece of her is part of the reason that I fell in love so quickly and completely. But that does not make me her.

She is not who I am. The girl in the mirror is not Livia.

I close my eyes because although Raine might understand that with his head, until his heart understands, I can't make this work.

"Hey." His hands press against my shoulders and I look into the mirror to see him behind me, his lips brushing my hair. "You're crying."

It's only when he says the words that I realize they are true.

"I'm sorry." I draw a breath and turn to face him because this isn't something I can say to his reflection. "I love you, Raine. Maybe it's been fast, or maybe it's been growing over centuries. I don't know and I don't care, because I am certain of how I feel."

I watch the smile bloom on his face, only to die with my next words.

"But you're not in love with me. You're in love with a memory, Raine."

He shakes his head. "No."

I take his hand and hold it tight. "I can't do this. I'm not Livia. Maybe a part of me was, but that was a long time ago, and I have no memory of it. Not really. Do I feel a connection to you? Do I love you? Desperately. Passionately. But I'm not going to reduce the truth of that feeling by saying it originates from another woman's past. It doesn't Raine. It's me. All me."

He watches me intently, but says nothing, and I press on, because I have to get this out.

"Maybe there is some of her in me, but it's no more than the atoms of dinosaurs. You talked about energy, and I understand that. Everything is connected, sure. Energy can be neither created nor destroyed. I get all of that, and it's part of why I believe that what you've told me is true. But I can't be some other person simply because that's who you lost so long ago and who you want me to be."

"That's not what I want." He is speaking carefully, as if a wrong step will send me away.

But he doesn't realize that I'm already gone. What matters now is whether he can get me back.

I take his hand. "Isn't it? The woman you loved is dead, Raine. I'm Callie, and I do love you. God, I love you so much it terrifies me. But that isn't enough to keep me here."

"What are you saying?"

"I'm saying I can't stay here. Because I can't be somebody else, Raine. Not even for love." I brush away a tear and draw a stuttering breath. "Not even for you."

* * * *

Raine couldn't sleep. He'd paced his apartment all night after Callie left, finally giving up even as the dark surrendered to the light.

He'd come down into the club an hour ago and decided that seven in the morning was a damn fine time for a drink.

Now he filled his glass yet again, then tossed back the contents, relishing the burn as the liquid flowed down his throat. He couldn't get drunk—a side effect of his particular brand of immortality—but he could damn sure try. And maybe if he tried hard enough he could turn the buzz into an alcohol-induced haze.

And maybe if he managed that, he could forget.

Except, of course, he didn't want to forget. On the contrary, he wanted to hold her close to his heart. Hold them. Both of the women he loved. His Livia. His Callie.

How the hell had he lost them both?

"Careful." Mal stepped up to the bar, then leaned against it, the casualness of his stance belying the concern on his face. "Finish off the Glenfarclas and Trace will have your head. He was friends with John Grant, you know, and was there when it was distilled. Not to mention that bottle cost a fucking fortune."

Raine managed a small smile. "Trace has wanted my head for centuries. About time I gave him an excuse."

"Don't do him any favors." Mal reached over the bar and grabbed a glass of his own, then held it out. "And don't drink alone."

Raine lifted the bottle and poured a shot into Mal's glass.

"She thinks that I'm in love with a memory."

Mal took a long, slow sip. "Are you?"

Raine's eyes shot to his friend, and his words came out cold and harsh. "Hell no. Christ, Mal, I loved Livia—I did. I do. And whatever part of her is still within Callie, I love as well. But that isn't why I love her. God, she's in here." He slammed his hand against his chest. "In my heart, under my skin. There was a spark the moment I saw her, and when we made love the first time, I knew without a doubt that I've known her forever—and maybe I do have Livia to thank for that—but it's not what's in our past that grabbed my heart."

His friend said nothing as Raine poured another shot, then finished it off. "Livia was my mate, and I loved her beyond all reason." He had, too. But they had been mated before they crossed the void, and that relationship had a different feel, a different cadence. They'd been bound, their energies meshed. And he had been sworn to protect her, while she was sworn to serve him.

The relationship was symbiotic, and yet sterile in so many ways. And perhaps they would have grown past that in their years on earth, bound in human flesh for so long that he'd all but forgotten how it used to be. But he'd lost her the day of their arrival, and so he would never know.

With Callie, he understood what it meant to not only love, but to be in love. To feel not only passion, but playfulness.

He had loved, Livia. But with Callie it was so much more. With Callie, *he* was so much more.

"I loved her," Raine repeated. "But Callie is a partner, too. A friend. Perhaps there was no room for that so many years ago, when our mission was so closely bound to every moment of our lives. But I found laughter in Callie. And life, as well. And if I have any regrets, it is my recklessness over these past years."

He rubbed a hand over his tattooed arm, remembering each and every death that they marked. "Because now I fear that if I go into battle and fail, I may lose myself. And in losing myself, I will lose her as well."

Still, his friend said nothing.

"Dammit, Mal, say something."

Mal reached over and clenched his shoulder, his gray eyes sharp. "It's not me you need to be talking to, Raine. And you damn well know it."

* * * *

It's nine in the morning and I'm on my fifth cup of coffee. I didn't sleep last night, though I'd curled up on the couch in my father's hospital room and hoped that the beeps and chirps of the machinery would sing me to sleep. I'd wanted to find my father in dreams, but it hadn't happened, and now I feel bereft, as if I'd lost both my father and the man I loved.

I'd left with the sun, walking back to the store as the city awoke, and as soon as the clock struck nine, I'd called my office in Texas.

Now I'm on hold because I'd foolishly forgotten about the time change, and the receptionist told me to wait while she calls down to the gym to see if my boss is there, going through his usual early-morning workout.

I'd considered simply calling back later, but I want to do this now. I want to let him know that I'll be back to work bright and early Monday morning, and I want him to officially put me back on the docket as soon as possible.

I force myself not to think about the reason. About why it even matters to me. Because I do not want to even entertain the possibility of staying in New York. How can I when everything about this city reminds me of Raine?

And all I do is remind him of Livia.

Frustrated, I wipe away a tear that has escaped my cheek.

He didn't stop me.

I told him what I needed to hear, and he said nothing. He let me walk out and keep on walking. And now it's the next day and he hasn't come, and dammit I can't help the stupid tears because my heart is broken. And I'm cursing my own stupidity for falling in love in the first place, and I'm wishing there is a way that I can just get him out of my head, because whenever I think about him—

Fuck.

"Dammit, Claire, get back to the phone." I tap my foot, then start pacing. I've reached the end of the store when two things happen. The front door opens and Raine steps in, and Claire comes back on the line.

"Just another minute," she says. "He's on his way up."

"Thanks. I can wait." I look up at Raine as the hold music begins again. I clutch my fingers tighter around my phone, as if that alone can give me the strength not to run to him. "My boss. I need to take this."

"Later. We need to talk."

I shake my head. "We don't."

"Yes." He moves closer, then takes the phone from my hand and disconnects the call. "We do. Because I love you. *You*. Callie Sinclair. Not a memory. A woman."

"It's been hours," I say because, yes, I am hurting. "You let me leave. You let me just walk away."

"I needed to get my head around how much I feel for you. Because it's so much more than I've ever felt before. For Livia. For anyone."

I look at him, wary, because I want so much to believe, but I don't know if I should.

On the desk, my phone starts to ring. I know it's Claire, wondering what the hell happened.

"No," he says. "Give me this chance to tell you that I love Callie Sinclair. That I want nothing more than to touch her. To make memories with her. I want to laugh with her and I want to watch her cry out in passion. I love you, Callie. Your humor, your heart. Everything that makes up the woman standing in front of me."

He pauses only long enough to draw a breath.

"Is Livia's essence within you? Of course. Did I love her? I did. But that was a long time ago, and now her essence is only the string that drew me to you. Strings can be cut. But you could sever that string and I would never leave you. *Never*," he adds fiercely. "You are everything to me, angel. Don't you see? For centuries, I've craved death. Sought it out. Wanted to find that goddamn amulet so that I could go back home, even though that world no longer is mine. I don't want that anymore."

He takes my hands. "I want to stay. I want you."

I swallow and blink, trying to hold back tears because his words have filled me to overflowing.

"I love you, Callie. And I'm sorry if I'm saying it wrong, but I need you to believe me. Because you hold the power to destroy me. Please, angel." His voice is gentle. Pleading. "I need you."

"I believe you," I say, and I don't think I've ever spoken truer words. "And I love you, too."

Chapter 11

"I love you," I say again, because it is real and huge and I want to say it as many times as he wants to hear it.

He pulls me close and kisses me hard. "I was so afraid I'd lost you forever, and—"

I close my mouth over his again, silencing him. I don't want to hear about being apart now that we are together. That, to me, is the wrong kind of fantasy.

"Make love to me." I'm breathing hard, my heart pounding. His is too, and as he pulls me close I can feel it pound through me as if our two hearts are united as one. As if we are blurring the line between where I end and he begins.

His hands go to my shirt even as mine attack his jeans. "The windows," I gasp, though right then I truly don't care. He can slam me up against the glass and fuck me blind if he wants. I just want to feel him against me.

In one motion, he scoops me up. "Where?"

"The studio. Upstairs." I nod to the back of the store and the simple door that leads the way to the living quarters. He goes, carrying me easily, and I cling tight, reveling in the feel of his body pressed against mine. Of being carried. Tended to. It feels right, this moment.

It feels like coming home.

I tense, realizing something.

"Callie?"

I make a frantic motion with my hand. "Wait. Wait. Let me think."

He continues up the stairs, his expression wary, but I say nothing. There's something important, and though it's flitting around in my mind, I can't quite grasp it no matter how much I—

And then I remember.

"My playhouse," I say, twisting my hand into his shirt collar as if that will make him understand what I'm talking about. "I think Daddy hid the amulet in my playhouse."

His brow creases. "What does that have to do with me? The journal said, *With him, what is hidden will be revealed.* I don't even know what your playhouse is."

"But you're with me, aren't you?"

He cocks his head. "And you think your dad knew that we would be together?"

"If Livia is in him, too, then yes. I think maybe he knew—maybe *she* knew—that in the end, we would make this work."

We've reached the landing at the top of the stairs and he pauses outside the door to the studio, then puts me down.

"What?" I ask because he is looking at me with such intensity.

"I just love you." His voice is gentle but firm, as if he has just stated some immutable law of the universe. And when he kisses me, threads of fire spread through me, filling and warming me, making me feel safe. And, yes, loved.

I have no idea what I said to prompt this, but I do know that I like it.

"So if it's in the playhouse, where is the playhouse?"

I reach for the door to the studio and open it. It's a typical loft apartment with no isolated rooms. My father put up a bookshelf to separate my area from his when I got older, but before that it was just open.

The back wall is made up of windows in front of a wooden bench. It's not a window seat, and that had disappointed me as a child. Until my dad decided to take pity on me.

I signal for Raine to come over, and he does. Then I kneel in front of the bench. I run my finger along the bottom until I find the hidden latch. I flip it, then lift the wooden panel. It rises on the hinges hidden just under the top to reveal a cavity just barely big enough for a little girl to use as a playhouse. Inside, I find my stuffed animals, a blanket, three flashlights, a pillow, a copy of *Alice in Wonderland*. And a cardboard box that I do not recognize.

I tug it out, then glance at Raine, who nods.

I pull off the lid, then suck in a breath, awed by the magnificent fire of the opal that makes up the center of the amulet. "It's stunning," I say. "Hang on. Let me get my dad's jeweler's loupe. The fire in this stone is incredible."

I clutch the box in my hand, intending to just run down the stairs and get my dad's loupe out of his desk, but I don't get that far.

The moment I step outside the door, I hear a sharp *crack*. For a moment, I just stand there, confused. Then I hear Raine scream my name. I try to turn, but I seem glued to the spot. And, strangely, when I look down I see blood on my shirt.

My blood.

I fall backward, realizing as I do that someone has leapt from the stairs to the landing. He's grabbed the box, and he's racing away.

I try to focus on why that matters, but everything just seems so fuzzy. Even Raine, who is at my side now, his hand tight around mine.

"Hang on!" he cries. "Dammit, Callie, you hang on."

But I'm not sure how he expects me to do that, because everything is so slippery, and I'm sliding away faster and faster.

"Don't you dare. Don't you dare leave me."

I focus on his words. On their meaning. And as I do, I realize what's happening.

Dying.

"Raine? I think I've been shot. I think I'm dying."

I see the tears flood his eyes and the way his jaw clenches with determination, and I know that I am right.

I try to shake my head, but I'm not sure I'm managing it. But when I shift sideways, I can scoot just a little bit closer to him. I can't stand to be away from him. I can't stand to lose him now that I've just found him.

"Raine?" My voice is so thin I can barely hear it. "I don't think I can hold on. I love you."

I think I am hallucinating now because I see a wild flash of colors. Then I realize it's not a hallucination. It's the blade of a fire sword.

"You said I could watch you forge it."

"This is Mal's. I also said I never go out without one. Listen to me. *Listen to me.*"

I force myself to focus. To not let the gray take me.

"They have...the amulet," I say.

"Right now, I don't give a damn about anything but you. I need you to move. I won't be able to do it for you once I slice my throat, and the fire will throw me across the room if I die too close to you. It won't risk accidentally taking a mortal. One foot, Callie. Can you crawl one foot into the flames?"

His words are coming at me fast, and I can barely process them. But I have heard enough, and it is the surge of adrenaline that gives me more strength because I have to make him stop. "Die? The flame? What are you talking about?"

"Come into the flame with me. If my mate enters, she will become immortal, too. Come into the flame, Callie, and live with me forever."

"No. Raine, *no.* You said you didn't have many burns left. This could destroy you."

The words, ripped from me in fear, have exhausted me, and I let my head fall back as I gasp, trying to draw in air.

"I can't bear to lose you," he says. "And if the price of your life is my sanity, then I will pay it to know that you are safe and whole."

I open my mouth to protest once more, but it is too late. He holds the base of the fire sword and with one flick of his wrist, the blade extends, slicing across his throat and spilling his blood.

I hear a scream and realize that it is my own.

He falls to the floor, and for a moment nothing happens.

"Raine… Raine…" I try to scream his name, but I do not have the strength.

He is facing me, and I see the light dimming in his eyes. And then his lips move. Just one word.

Now.

The word still hangs in the air as the flames start to rise around him. And I know that I must go now. The flame will not last forever, only until he is reborn.

I either try or I die.

And I cannot bear the thought of losing him. And so I struggle toward him, using all my strength. Pushing with my feet. Pulling with my arms. Until I am so close I can feel the fire cooking my skin, and I do not know how I can do this. How I can go into the flame and suffer that pain?

Except I know that I can endure it because Raine has, time and again. And twice now for me.

I can survive it for him.

I count to three, then force my body to roll, screaming in pain as I do from both the pressure on the wound and the fire that has now sparked my clothes. But that is good, I think, because I need the flame. I need to burn. I need…

I need…

And then there is just black. Black and pain.

Then something soothing. And a light. Blue and yellow and a deep, blood red.

Shining. Healing. And rising into the sky on jeweled wings.

Illusion? Or reality? Or is there even a difference?

I do not know. I don't even know if I am alive or dead.

All I know is that the pain has stopped but the black has come. So deep and thick that I know that Raine was wrong. This is the end.
This is death.
And death is cold and black.

* * * *

"*Time to wake up, sweetheart.*"
"*Daddy?*"
I'm surrounded by black, the floor beneath me cold and hard.
"*You did good. You found the amulet.*"
I search for him, but there is only his voice and the black.
"*We lost it.*"
"*You survived. You're alive. And you're with Raine.*"
"*I love him, Daddy.*"
"*I know. And I love you.*"
"*I miss you.*"
"*I'm here. But right now, Callie, you need to leave this place. Follow the path, Callie,*" *he says, his voice fading as a faint, golden path seems to shine on the floor.*
"*Daddy?*"
I reach for him, but he's gone, his voice drifting away down the path. I crawl that direction, and as I do, the blackness turns to gray, and then the gray turns to light.

And I open my eyes.

I'm on the floor of the studio, gasping and naked in Raine's arms.

I look down at my chest, right were the bullet got me, so close to my heart. The skin is completely unmarred.

Beside me, Raine stirs, blue eyes overflowing with relief. And with love.

"We're really safe?" I ask. "We're really alive? Are you okay?" And not just alive, but immortal. The thought is still too big for my head, though I am certain that if I am going to tackle immortality, I want to do it with Raine beside me.

"I am. We are." He brushes his hand over my hair, his eyes still focused on my face as if he can't believe I am here.

I understand completely. "Make love to me," I beg. "Please, Raine. Please prove to me that I'm really alive."

"Oh, angel, you're alive. More alive than you've ever been." He brushes his hand over the curve of my shoulder, his expression filled with awe.

I look too, and when I see the vibrant, colorful phoenix tattoo my breath hitches and I feel something that I would call joy, except that the feeling is too big to fit into such a small word. "It's true? I'm really immortal?"

"It's true," he says, but I do not really need his answer. I can feel it. This new energy swirling inside me. The connection that I have sought for so long. And the full feeling inside me that has completely conquered that horrible sense of emptiness.

Raine.

He is my mate, my love, my life.

And I will never be alone.

"You're smiling," he says.

"I have reason to." I shift on the ground so that I am straddling him. The floor is hard, but I don't care. I'm desperate for him, overwhelmed with the need for our bodies to prove what my heart already knows. That this is real. That this is forever. And that this man is a part of me.

I move my hips in a slow motion. "Let me give you a reason to smile too," I say huskily.

I see passion light those ice-blue eyes. "Angel, I'm already smiling."

He pulls me close and closes his mouth over mine. The kiss is wild and deep and bruising. I don't care. I want the bruises. I've already got the tattoo, now I want to be marked by Raine as well. Marked by him. Filled by him. Taken by him.

I feel wild—hell, I feel alive—and I break the kiss and then sit up, stroking his hard, thick cock even as I rise up on my knees and position his head at my slit, and then lower myself slowly, so painfully slowly, so that I am teasing us both.

"You're killing me, angel," he says, and then takes hold of my back with one hand and my rear with the other, and in a surprisingly fluid movement, flips us.

Now I'm on my back and he is on his knees. And I'm gasping with pleasure as he holds my hips and pistons into me, hard and fast and deep.

He is taking me higher and higher, and we are joined now, body and soul. And when I explode in a thousand pieces, he is right there, too, merging with me, dancing with me, filling me completely.

When we both finally come back to earth, I snuggle close, my head on his chest. He reaches into the playhouse for the blanket and pulls it over us.

I frown, remembering what else was in that playhouse. "I'm sorry about the amulet."

"We'll get it back. It's as useless to them as it is to us without all seven pieces."

"Thank goodness."

I sigh and press closer to him, then trail my finger over the tats that mark his chest. "So am I different now? After the fire, I mean?"

"You're immortal, like me. Other than that, you are still you."

I smile again, both amazed and content that I will never leave this man. But something in his words makes me wonder. "Does that mean you're more than immortal? Do you have powers or something?" I feel a little silly asking, as if I'm trying to turn him into a comic book hero. I expect him to laugh off the question, so his answer startles me.

"You might say that."

I sit up. "Really? More than your power to make me feel very, very good?"

He laughs. "Energy. Within certain limitations, we can manipulate it."

I frown, trying to understand. And then I remember. "That first day. I *did* lock the door."

"It's an electronic keypad lock. I simply told it to open."

"That is pretty damn cool."

"What can I say? I'm a very cool guy."

I roll over and kiss him again. "You're a hell of a lot more than that," I say. "You're *my* cool guy."

"I am," he says. "Forever."

He strokes my hair and looks into my eyes, and the tenderness in his gaze makes me melt all over again.

"I love you," I whisper.

"And I love you."

"Make love to me, Raine. Slow and long. I want to feel you inside me. I never want to stop feeling you."

"Anything you want, angel." He brushes my lips with a tender kiss. "We have all the time in the world."

Epilogue

Mal continued to study the chessboard as Liam dropped into the seat across the table from him, then put his phone down.

"Just heard from Raine. Callie's now a New York County Assistant District Attorney."

"That's excellent," Mal said as he considered the position of the rook in relation to the bishop. "It can only help Phoenix Security to have someone in the DA's office."

"Agreed," Liam said, and then said nothing else.

Mal closed his eyes, silently cursing, then looked up. "Something else?"

"I don't know. Is there?"

Mal said nothing, just waited.

"Dammit, Mal, you need to talk to me. You've been brooding for two days, sitting over this damn chessboard, half the time without an opponent."

"There's always an opponent," Mal said.

"Jessica's worried."

At that, Mal bit back a smile. "Jessica?"

"Fine. I'm worried, too. Tell me I don't have reason to be."

Mal sighed, then combed his fingers through his hair. "I've been thinking about games. About strategies."

"Mal. Don't do this to yourself."

"To myself?" A sudden fury burst through him, and he lashed out, sending chess pieces flying. "Do you think I want this pain? Dammit, Liam, not a day goes by that I don't think of her. That I don't crave the moment when I will see her again...even as I dread it."

Liam drew in a breath. "I wish I didn't have to tell you this. But she's back. She's in New York. "

Mal's body turned to ice. "Are you sure?"

"Dante saw her. She was at least a block away, so he could be wrong, but—"

"He's not," Mal said flatly as the cold settled into his bones. He turned his attention to the now empty chessboard.

"Do you think it doesn't destroy me, too? She was your mate, but she was my friend, my crew. But there's no other way," Liam said, accurately following Mal's thoughts. "There is no other strategy, no trick we haven't thought of. There is only one way."

He stood, and Mal could see the pain on his friend's face, as potent as his own. "You have to kill her again, Mal. Because if you don't, she'll end up destroying us all."

Sign up for the 1001 Dark Nights Newsletter
and be entered to win a Tiffany Key necklace.

There's a new contest every month!

Go to www.DarkNights.com to subscribe.

As a bonus, all subscribers will receive a free
1001 Dark Nights story
The First Night
by Lexi Blake & M.J. Rose

Turn the page for a full list of the
1001 Dark Nights fabulous novellas...

1001 Dark Nights

WICKED WOLF by Carrie Ann Ryan
A Redwood Pack Novella

WHEN IRISH EYES ARE HAUNTING by Heather Graham
A Krewe of Hunters Novella

EASY WITH YOU by Kristen Proby
A With Me In Seattle Novella

MASTER OF FREEDOM by Cherise Sinclair
A Mountain Masters Novella

CARESS OF PLEASURE by Julie Kenner
A Dark Pleasures Novella

ADORED by Lexi Blake
A Masters and Mercenaries Novella

HADES by Larissa Ione
A Demonica Novella

RAVAGED by Elisabeth Naughton
An Eternal Guardians Novella

DREAM OF YOU by Jennifer L. Armentrout
A Wait For You Novella

STRIPPED DOWN by Lorelei James
A Blacktop Cowboys ® Novella

RAGE/KILLIAN by Alexandra Ivy/Laura Wright
Bayou Heat Novellas

DRAGON KING by Donna Grant
A Dark Kings Novella

PURE WICKED by Shayla Black
A Wicked Lovers Novella

HARD AS STEEL by Laura Kaye
A Hard Ink/Raven Riders Crossover

STROKE OF MIDNIGHT by Lara Adrian
A Midnight Breed Novella

ALL HALLOWS EVE by Heather Graham
A Krewe of Hunters Novella

KISS THE FLAME by Christopher Rice
A Desire Exchange Novella

DARING HER LOVE by Melissa Foster
A Bradens Novella

TEASED by Rebecca Zanetti
A Dark Protectors Novella

THE PROMISE OF SURRENDER by Liliana Hart
A MacKenzie Family Novella

FOREVER WICKED by Shayla Black
A Wicked Lovers Novella

CRIMSON TWILIGHT by Heather Graham
A Krewe of Hunters Novella

CAPTURED IN SURRENDER by Liliana Hart
A MacKenzie Family Novella

SILENT BITE: A SCANGUARDS WEDDING by Tina
Folsom
A Scanguards Vampire Novella

DUNGEON GAMES by Lexi Blake
A Masters and Mercenaries Novella

AZAGOTH by Larissa Ione
A Demonica Novella

NEED YOU NOW by Lisa Renee Jones
A Shattered Promises Series Prelude

SHOW ME, BABY by Cherise Sinclair
A Masters of the Shadowlands Novella

ROPED IN by Lorelei James
A Blacktop Cowboys ® Novella

TEMPTED BY MIDNIGHT by Lara Adrian
A Midnight Breed Novella

THE FLAME by Christopher Rice
A Desire Exchange Novella

CARESS OF DARKNESS by Julie Kenner
A Dark Pleasures Novella

Also from Evil Eye Concepts:

TAME ME by J. Kenner
A Stark International Novella

THE SURRENDER GATE By Christopher Rice
A Desire Exchange Novel

A BOUQUET FROM M. J. ROSE
A bundle including 6 novels and 1 short story collection

Bundles:
BUNDLE ONE
Includes Forever Wicked by Shayla Black
Crimson Twilight by Heather Graham
Captured in Surrender by Liliana Hart
Silent Bite by Tina Folsom

Acknowledgments from the Author

For Liz and Kim … who jumped through hoops and bent over backwards and saved my sanity in the process!

About Julie Kenner

J. Kenner (aka Julie Kenner) is the *New York Times*, *USA Today*, *Publishers Weekly*, *Wall Street Journal* and International bestselling author of over seventy novels, novellas and short stories in a variety of genres.

Though known primarily for her award-winning and international bestselling erotic romances (including the Stark and Most Wanted series) that have reached as high as #2 on the *New York Times* bestseller list, JK has been writing full time for over a decade in a variety of genres including paranormal and contemporary romance, "chicklit" suspense, urban fantasy, Victorian-era thrillers (coming soon), and paranormal mommy lit.

Her foray into the latter, *Carpe Demon: Adventures of a Demon-Hunting Soccer Mom* by Julie Kenner, has been consistently in development in Hollywood since prior to publication. Most recently, it has been optioned by Warner Brothers Television for development as series on the CW Network with Alloy Entertainment producing.

JK has been praised by *Publishers Weekly* as an author with a "flair for dialogue and eccentric characterizations" and by *RT Bookclub* for having "cornered the market on sinfully attractive, dominant antiheroes and the women who swoon for them." A three time finalist for Romance Writers of America's prestigious RITA award, JK took home the first RITA trophy awarded in the category of erotic romance in 2014 for her novel, *Claim Me* (book 2 of her Stark Trilogy).

Her books have sold well over a million copies and are published in over over twenty countries.

In her previous career as an attorney, JK worked as a clerk on the Fifth Circuit Court of Appeals, and practiced primarily civil, entertainment and First Amendment litigation in Los Angeles and Irvine, California, as well as in Austin, Texas. She currently lives in Central Texas, with her husband, two daughters, and two rather spastic cats.

Dark Pleasures

Don't miss the next novellas in the Dark Pleasures series!

Mal and Christina's story coming in January, Find Me in Darkness, Find Me in Pleasure, and Find Me in Passion…

A doomed woman. A dangerous and mysterious man. And an epic passion that cannot be denied…

Learn more at Julie's website: http://bit.ly/DarkPleasures

Also from Julie Kenner

Erotic romance

<u>As Julie Kenner</u>
Caress of Darkness
Find Me in Darkness
Find Me in Pleasure
Find Me in Passion
Caress of Pleasure

<u>As J. Kenner</u>
Stark Series novels
Release Me (a *New York Times* and *USA Today* bestseller)
Claim Me (a #2 *New York Times* bestseller!)
Complete Me (a #2 *New York Times* bestseller!)

Stark Ever After novellas
Take Me
Have Me
Play My Game

Stark International novels
Say My Name
On My Knees
Under My Skin

Stark International novellas
Tame Me

The Most Wanted series
Wanted
Heated
Ignited

Other Genres
Kate Connor Demon-Hunting Soccer Mom Series (suburban
fantasy/paranormal)
Carpe Demon
California Demon
Demons Are Forever
The Demon You Know (short story)
Deja Demon
Demon Ex Machina
Pax Demonica

The Protector (Superhero) Series (paranormal romance)
The Cat's Fancy (prequel)
Aphrodite's Kiss
Aphrodite's Passion
Aphrodite's Secret
Aphrodite's Flame
Aphrodite's Embrace
Aphrodite's Delight
Aphrodite's Charms (boxed set)

Blood Lily Chronicles (urban fantasy romance)
Tainted
Torn
Turned
The Blood Lily Chronicles (boxed set)

Devil May Care Series (paranormal romance)
Raising Hell
Sure As Hell

Shadow Keepers Series (J. Kenner writing as J.K. Beck)
When Blood Calls
When Pleasure Rules
When Wicked Craves
Shadow Keepers: Midnight (e-novella)
When Passion Lies
When Darkness Hungers
When Temptation Burns

On behalf of 1001 Dark Nights,
Liz Berry and M.J. Rose would like to thank ~

Doug Scofield
Steve Berry
Richard Blake
Dan Slater
Asha Hossain
Chris Graham
Kim Guidroz
BookTrib After Dark
Jillian Stein
and Simon Lipskar

Printed in the USA
CPSIA information can be obtained
at www.ICGtesting.com
JSHW031705140824
68134JS00036B/3526